"You're beautiful," he whispered.

"So are you," she murmured. "Oh, Max, please…"

"Please what?" he asked huskily, sliding the jacket off her shoulders and tossing it on to the floor.

"Please kiss me," she said.

He caught her wrists, pulled them against his thighs and stared down at her. "Faith," he said softly, "do you mean…?"

"Oh, yes," breathed Faith. "Yes, yes, yes. Please…"

With a muffled laugh, because his mouth was pressed against her hair, Max scooped her up in his arms and bore her out into the living room.

"I—I've only a single bed," she murmured.

"Not an insuperable barrier…"

Kay Gregory grew up in England but moved to Canada as a teenager, and now lives with her husband in Vancouver. They have two sons who have now moved away, along with two ferrets, leaving them sole custodians of the family dog. Kay has had more jobs than she can possibly remember, the best of which is writing Harlequin romance novels.

Look out for *The Heat of the Moment* later this year, in which we meet again some of the characters in this story.

Books by Kay Gregory

Man of the Mountains
Kay Gregory

Harlequin Books

**TORONTO • NEW YORK • LONDON
AMSTERDAM • PARIS • SYDNEY • HAMBURG
STOCKHOLM • ATHENS • TOKYO • MILAN
MADRID • WARSAW • BUDAPEST • AUCKLAND**

TO: My agent, Irene Goodman,
with gratitude for all her help and support.

ISBN 0-373-17276-1

MAN OF THE MOUNTAINS

First North American Publication 1996.

CHAPTER ONE

SHE didn't look crazy, Max decided. At a glance she seemed a rather ordinary, could-be-pretty-if-she-bothered country blonde. Only there was nothing ordinary about a slender young woman in a conservative navy blue suit sitting on a log at the edge of the ocean playing the banjo. Not when the yellow-tinged clouds overhead held promise of an April downpour, and the wind whistling past her ears was lifting her long hair so that it fell across her face like tangled silk.

She looked utterly incongruous. Prim conventionality gone mad.

Max found her enchanting.

He wondered what would happen if he spoke to her. Was he likely, for his pains, to get a handful of sand in the face? This was an isolated stretch of beach, and she was a modern miss who had doubtless been taught not to talk to strangers.

He thrust his tongue into his cheek and crunched across the pebbles to where she sat. He might be a stranger, but *she* was the strange one. He would risk it. He had risked a lot worse than sand in his life and faced obstacles far more threatening than this unusual slip of a girl.

If Faith had been less engrossed in her playing, she might have heard him approach. As it was, when her fingers on the strings stilled briefly, and a warm male voice behind her said, 'Good evening, Euterpe,' she jumped.

'My name's not Euterpe,' she replied, throwing her head back and continuing her rhythmic strumming.

Max knew he was safe from the sand.

'Maybe not,' he acknowledged. 'Euterpe was a daughter of Zeus, the Muse of Music. You remind me of her.'

Faith stopped playing and turned to look at him, her pale violet gaze undiscomfited. 'Is that so? Nice line, Mr...?'

'Kain—Maxwell Kain.'

She nodded, unimpressed. 'Mr Kain. As I said, nice line. I haven't heard it before.'

She saw irritation expand the muscles of his chest, which was covered only by a thin blue sweatshirt and a black windbreaker. 'I'm sorry you don't appreciate Greek mythology,' he said curtly.

Faith smiled, noting the tight look around his mouth and admiring, in a clinical fashion, the masculine perfection of his features. No, on second thoughts, not perfection. From the looks of it, his nose had been broken at one time, and his skin exposed routinely to the elements. It was a farmer's skin, tough, bronzed. Only he didn't look like a farmer. The expression in his grey eyes was too visionary. Rooted in sweat perhaps, but not in soil. Apart from that, he had a strong, stubborn chin and a solid neck, and his light brown hair curled nicely above his ears. Attractive. Mid-thirties probably. Not overly tall, but the sort of man you wouldn't miss in a crowd.

'I majored in Classics,' she told him mildly, and felt a fragile bubble of triumph when she saw his eyebrows lift and his full lips press together in surprise. This man was a little too patronising, she decided. He didn't like being one-upped, and he was too sure of his own appeal. She had been through more than enough of that with Stephen.

But Maxwell Kain wasn't Stephen.

For a moment he stood over her looking a bit like Euterpe's father, then he shrugged and murmured with a wry, unexpectedly attractive smile, 'I might have guessed.'

Faith shifted her banjo to her right hand as, without being asked, he sat down on the log beside her. 'What might you have guessed?'

'That a woman as mysterious as you are would have graduated from school with qualifications beyond typing and hormones.'

'I am a typist,' she said coldly. 'I was recently cured of hormones by a man very much like yourself, and I'm not in the least mysterious.'

Max frowned and ran a hand through his hair. She saw that it was so thick that the wind had scarcely disturbed it.

'Aren't you?' he said. His voice held traces of an accent she couldn't place. 'In that case tell me what you're doing sitting alone on a deserted beach in the middle of a howling gale, wearing a costume which would win nods of approval if you wore it to a business luncheon.'

Faith chuckled softly. 'Old Mr Rosenthal did nod— with approval, I suppose—when I wore it to lunch at the Clambake with my boss.'

He glanced at her sideways. Sleepy-looking eyelids lifted to expose wide-awake, very perceptive eyes. She could tell he was trying to make up his mind whether she was exceptionally obtuse or simply avoiding his question.

'I don't know anything about old Mr Rosenthal or your boss,' he said abruptly. 'What I *would* be interested in knowing is what you're doing here.'

'Playing my banjo.' She smiled innocently, then wondered if she had carried innocence too far, because this powerfully built man appeared to be suppressing a strong urge to take her by the scruff of the neck and hurl her and her banjo bodily into the waves.

'I can see that,' he said, with such controlled frustration that Faith laughed outright.

She had been told she had a musical laugh, but it didn't have the effect of soothing Maxwell Kain, who sat astride the log, removed the banjo from her hand, and placed it carefully over his knees. Then, taking her upper arms, he twisted her around to face him.

'OK,' he said. 'Name?'

Faith blinked. 'Name?'

'Yours. What are you called?'

'Is this an interrogation, Mr Kain?'

'I had hoped it would be a civilised conversation.'

'In that case, please take your hands off me.'

Max removed his hands and placed them on his thighs. Faith eyed them with wary respect. They were capable-looking hands, with strong, square-tipped fingers. His thighs looked capable too, firm and muscular. Not the thighs of a man who spent much time behind a desk.

'Right,' he said, 'let's start again. Your name isn't Euterpe, so what is it?'

Faith bit her lip. His assumption that he had a right to know annoyed her, but, contrarily, she wanted to tell him. There was something compelling, almost mesmeric, about those far-seeing light grey eyes. Elsewhere eyes, she thought dreamily.

'It's Faith,' she said, after a long pause. 'Faith Farraday.'

He put his head to one side. 'Hmm. Yes, there's a certain music in that. I think it suits you.'

'So glad you approve.' She tossed her head, and the wind caught at her hair.

'Oh, I do. But I don't much approve of sarcastic females. Do you live here in Caley Cove, then, Faith Farraday?'

'Yes,' said Faith. 'In a cave with my cat and a very long broomstick.'

'You don't listen well, do you?' His deep voice was soft as silk.

'What do you mean?'

'I said I don't like sarcastic females. Although the cat and the broomstick wouldn't altogether surprise me.'

Faith frowned, annoyed and very disturbed to discover that his criticism hit a raw nerve. There wasn't the remotest reason why it should. This man's opinion meant nothing to her. 'If you must know,' she said, deciding it wasn't worth while sparring with him, 'I do live here in Caley Cove. I'm a very ordinary country girl, Mr Kain. Sarcastic, too. Not your type, I'm afraid.'

'Oh, I don't know.' He let his leisurely gaze wander across her face, then down her slender neck and over her breasts and hips. When he came to long, silk-covered legs that ended in neat navy pumps, he said, 'I think you'll do.'

Faith stood up, her shoes sinking into the sand. 'Unfortunately I'm not auditioning for the part. Can I have my banjo, please? I have to go.'

He shifted along the log, drawing her eyes to the muscular expanse of his legs. 'Why?'

She swallowed, feeling an uncomfortable stirring deep inside her body. 'Why? Because—because I'm cold, and it's suppertime.' When that failed to wipe the faint look of amusement off his face, she added hastily, 'Besides, it's starting to rain.'

Max looked up in time to see a large drop land on her nose. 'So it is,' he agreed, not moving. 'Which brings me to my original question. What the devil were you doing sitting alone on the beach with a major storm coming in over the ocean?'

'If I answer that, will you give me back my banjo?'

He grinned suddenly. 'Why not try it and see?'

Faith pressed her lips together. 'All right,' she agreed, trying not to notice how seductive he looked when he smiled. 'If you must know, I live in Caley Cove's one and only apartment block, and grouchy Mrs Gruber downstairs complains that my playing disturbs her. But it helps me unwind after work, and as there's never anyone on the beach at this time of year...' She stopped, glared at him, and muttered under her breath, 'Until today... I usually walk down here to enjoy an uninterrupted hour with my music.'

Max ignored the glare, and several more drops of rain, and said sternly, 'You shouldn't. The nearest house is half a mile away. What would you do if someone like me attacked you?'

'Were you thinking of it?' she asked sweetly.

'No.'

'I didn't think so.'

'That, Miss Farraday, is not the point. You have no way of knowing when some scumbag with intentions much less honourable than mine may take it into his head to follow you down the hill on your walk. In those clothes you couldn't hope to outrun him.'

Faith watched his windbreaker billow out around him like a sail, then deflate slowly as the coming gale paused to gather its breath. Max seemed oblivious to the cold, but she shivered slightly.

'In the first place,' she said, 'although I don't see that it's any of your business, I can't be bothered to change because I prefer to come here straight from work. In the second place, I don't need to run.'

'That's sheer lunacy. How can you possibly be sure?'

'Well, for one thing, Caley Cove has plenty of wagging tongues but, at present, no resident scumbags. And if you're talking about the occasional passing salesman or tourist—yourself, for instance—why don't you try attacking me and see?'

She put her hands on her hips and challenged him with her eyes.

Max laid the banjo down and rose slowly, and, in spite of her resentment, Faith couldn't help admiring the way he moved, with a lean lithe grace that was smooth and completely controlled.

'Is that an invitation?' he asked softly.

'Take it any way you like.' Surreptitiously she began to ease her foot out of her shoe.

But to her astonishment and relief, after fixing her with a provocative grey eye and flexing a nicely muscled forearm, quite suddenly Max threw his head back and let out a roar of laughter.

'You really would take me on, wouldn't you?' he gibed. 'I suppose you have a black belt in karate.'

Faith lowered her eyes. 'Not exactly,' she admitted, regretting her bravado, yet knowing somehow that from this man she had nothing to fear. Nothing physical, anyway. 'Just a yellow belt, in judo. But I've had to give it up since I left Seattle. There's no *dojo* here.'

Max ran a hand across his forehead in mock relief. 'In that case,' he said with a leer, 'why don't I get on with assaulting you?'

'Why don't you just give me back my banjo?' retorted Faith, who was finding herself oddly disconcerted by this strange encounter, and more than a little anxious to get away.

He bent to pick up the banjo, giving her a mouth-watering view of tight jeans stretching across his backside. 'Where's the case?' he asked peremptorily.

The clouds above them opened at that moment to deliver their burden in earnest. Faith pulled the case from behind the log, took the instrument from him and stowed it quickly away. Then she slipped her shoes off and, without looking back, began to run for the path that led up to the road.

'I'll give you a lift,' Max's voice shouted above the wind. 'You can't walk back to town in this.'

'Why can't I? A little rain won't hurt me.' She was panting by the time she reached the top.

'No, it'll only soak you to the skin. My car's just under those trees.'

'No, thank you,' said Faith firmly, as a gust of wind swept under her jacket. 'I don't mind walking.'

She felt his hand on her shoulder. 'Don't be a fool, Farraday. If I'd wanted to attack you I'd have done it down there on the beach.'

'I said no, thank you,' Faith repeated, not sure why she was so determined to do without his help, but certain it was the right thing to do. Not the sensible thing, perhaps, but she had always acted according to instinct, without giving much thought to the consequences, and more often than not her instinct had served her well.

As the rain fell in sheets around her head and shoulders, she marched ahead of Max up the hill.

'Oh, for crying out loud,' she heard him mutter close to her ear.

The next thing she knew, the banjo had been removed from her grasp.

She swung round, gasping, and immediately found herself suspended several feet above the ground in a pair of very powerful masculine arms. Without speaking Max strode to the passenger door of a smart silver-grey Ford, swung it open, and dumped her unceremoniously on the seat. The banjo landed beside her. Faith turned to get out again, but he slammed the door in her face and turned the key.

By the time she had located the inside catch, he was beside her, and the car was already purring up the hill.

'I suppose,' said Faith, pulling at her wet skirt so that it wouldn't cling so revealingly to her legs, 'that your concern for my safety from scumbags doesn't extend to my being kidnapped by hulking great gorillas.'

'Gorillas are essentially peaceful souls,' he said with his eyes on the road. 'And I'm not kidnapping you, I'm giving you a lift to prevent you from getting wet.'

'I didn't want a lift. And I'm already wet.'

'All right, *wetter*,' he said curtly. 'And I'm quite well aware that you didn't want a lift.'

His voice was surprisingly hard, and when Faith glanced sideways she decided his mouth wasn't nearly as attractive as she'd thought.

'Then why did you kidnap me?' she demanded.

'I didn't. I just couldn't stand to see an intelligent woman make a complete idiot of herself. A very wet idiot,' he added, with a glance at her saturated suit.

Faith subsided into her seat and didn't answer. Because he was right. She was in no more danger from him now than she had been down on the beach, and her refusal to accept his help had been based entirely on resentment of his high-handedness and a reluctance to get involved with another Stephen. Except that, for all his irritating assurance, she sensed that Maxwell Kain wasn't remotely like the suave and successful Stephen.

A few minutes later they came to the outskirts of town, and Max swerved to the right in front of a flat-roofed, cream stucco building with a narrow strip of grass along the front. The rest of the property was made up of concrete and cars. The Ford came to a stop with a very faint squeal of brakes.

'How did you know I live here?' asked Faith, breaking the silence only because she couldn't contain her curiosity.

'You said you lived in Caley Cove's only apartment block. I'm staying in its only hotel, and I've been exploring.'

'Oh.' She fumbled for the handle of the door, but he was already out, holding it for her. 'Thank you,' she mumbled as she edged past him and ran across the pavement to the porch.

But as she groped in her bag for her key, she became aware that Max was right behind her. She could feel his breath fanning her damp cheek.

'I said thank you for the lift,' she said, turning to face him, and finding that he was standing very close to her with his hands in his pockets and the rain dripping relentlessly down his face. She moved aside so he could shelter under the overhanging roof.

'Any time,' he said easily, resting his shoulders on the doorframe.

'You're standing in front of the keyhole,' Faith pointed out. When he didn't move she sighed and persisted, 'Mr Kain, it's raining, I'm cold, and I'd very much like to open this door.'

He shifted slightly, just enough so that she could fit her key in the lock. When she turned it, her hand brushed up against his hip. But he didn't move.

The door swung open. 'Thanks again,' said Faith, stepping inside. 'It—it was kind of you, even if——'

'Even if you would have greatly preferred to get soaked?' he suggested, lifting an eyebrow that was considerably darker than his hair.

She smiled, a little sheepishly. 'Mmm,' she admitted, 'as a matter of fact, I would.' She glanced down at the shoes she still held in her hand, and shuffled her sandy stockings on the floor preparatory to shutting the door in his face. But there was something in his eyes that made her hesitate. Something challenging and at the same time hypnotic.

'You're wet too,' she said inanely.

'I had noticed.'

'Had you? I was beginning to think you were oblivious to weather.' Faith shook off the odd effect of his eyes and forced herself to come back to earth.

'Not oblivious. In my business that can prove fatal. Has on occasions.'

Faith's curiosity sparked up again, but she had a feeling that, if she gave in to it, Maxwell Kain would end up getting what he wanted. Whatever that was.

'Well,' she said quickly, 'I have to get supper on now, so if you don't mind——'

'Supper?' he interrupted.

Faith saw his lips part in what she supposed was meant to be a hungry smile. 'Yes,' she said irritably, 'but if you think I shouldn't go alone to the beach, surely you don't expect me to entertain a stranger for supper?'

'Why not? If grouchy Mrs Gruber can hear you when you play your banjo, I'm sure she'd hear sounds of a sexual skirmish.'

He was looking at her with that butter-wouldn't-melt-in-his-mouth expression again, and Faith lowered her head because his talk of a sexual skirmish unaccountably made her feel shy. Which was ridiculous. She was twenty-six years old, not totally inexperienced, and she lived in a world where maidenly modesty was not regarded as an attribute. In fact it was considered remarkably old-fashioned.

'Mrs Gruber hears everything,' she acknowledged grudgingly. 'But she only interrupts when what I'm doing isn't something worth reporting to her friends.'

'Ah, I see. And you think she might find a lot of heavy breathing worth reporting?'

'I'm sure she would,' said Faith, surprised to find herself choking back a laugh.

'I get it. Unmarried tenant—you are unmarried, aren't you?—caught in compromising position with man and banjo. That sort of thing?'

His expression was completely deadpan, and Faith put a hand over her mouth to hide a smile. 'Yes, exactly that sort of thing,' she answered, staring resolutely down at the floor.

'And do you care? About Mrs Gruber?'

'No.'

'In that case, Miss Farraday, what's the problem?'

'The problem,' Faith began in exasperation, 'is that...' She stopped abruptly because when she looked up Max was lounging in the doorway with his thumbs hooked into his belt. And he was grinning at her—the sexiest grin she had ever seen in her life. She moistened her lips. What had she been about to say? She couldn't remember. 'I—I guess there isn't any problem,' she admitted in a strangled voice, as he settled his wide shoulders more comfortably. 'Do you—er—do you want to come in? I don't know what there is to eat, but——'

'I thought you'd never ask,' he cut in, stepping briskly into the small hallway and clicking the door shut behind him.

Faith turned to lead the way up the two flights of stairs to her apartment, all the time uneasily conscious that Max was behind her, more than likely with his eyes riveted on her clinging wet skirt.

She took the last few steps at a run. A minute later she flung open the door to her apartment and announced breathlessly, 'Here we are, then. My happy home.'

Max followed her across the threshold and stopped dead. 'If you say so,' he drawled, his deep voice expressing doubt and, if she was not much mistaken, disapproval.

'What's wrong with it?' she demanded.

'Nothing much. What do you use for furniture? Imagination?'

Faith bridled. 'I don't need a lot of furniture,' she informed him. 'There's a perfectly good carpet, and I always lie on cushions to watch TV. A whole lot of furniture is just a nuisance.'

'I see,' said Max, eyeing the bare mustard-coloured carpet with disfavour, and wondering if this extraordinary young woman with the heart-shaped face and softly curving mouth actually ate her meals off the floor. Or did she arrange that multi-coloured pile of cushions in the corner into something resembling a table?

Faith, catching the drift of his thoughts, said loftily, 'This isn't the whole of my apartment. I have a table in the kitchen. And a bed.'

'In the kitchen?' asked Max politely.

'No, of course not. In the bedroom.'

'Very appropriate,' he nodded, noting the indignant angle of her head.

Faith eyed him with deep scepticism, but his expression gave nothing away. She took a long breath. 'Yes, and now I'm going in there to change. You can use the bathroom if you like.'

'Thank you. And what do you suggest I change into?'

'What do you usually use for clothes?' Faith couldn't resist the chance to get her own back. 'Imagination?'

'If necessary.' His crooked smile left her wondering if she might have been better advised to keep her smart remarks to herself. She was still wondering when Max disappeared from the room.

After a moment's hesitation she turned and went into her bedroom.

This is crazy, she thought, peeling off her wet jacket and letting it drop to the floor. Stephen had often complained that she rarely stopped to think before she acted, but she had thought this time. And still ended up with Maxwell Kain masterminding a discreet but entirely successful invasion of her privacy. There was something very unstoppable about Max, something rugged, tough and persistent that bowled over obstacles almost as if they weren't there. She wondered what he did for a living, and remembered his comment that taking no account of weather could prove fatal. Was he a fisherman, then? A toiler of the sea? Somehow she didn't think so. Fish didn't go with those strange, faraway eyes.

She kicked off her skirt, picked up the jacket, and draped both of them over a rickety wooden chair. Then, after a cursory glance at the haphazard stack of boxes she used for drawers, she made for the big built-in cupboard beside the window and pulled out a rainbow-striped, tent-like garment made of soft brushed cotton. She put it on, and, after shaking out her wet hair and drying it perfunctorily with a towel, she made her way into the kitchen.

What now? she thought. Poached eggs on toast were all she had planned on eating after an extended lunch with Angela and Mr Rosenthal. But Max Kain had the look of a man who would require something more substantial than eggs.

Faith opened her fridge and was confronted by the cold back end of yesterday's barbecued chicken. It looked a bit tired, but with a bit of jazzing up it ought to do. If it didn't, Mr Kain would be speedily cured of inviting himself to dine with unknown women.

She began chopping up parsley, and was so absorbed in the job that she didn't realise Max was in the kitchen until a deep baritone behind her exclaimed, 'Good grief, what a transformation. From sober navy blue executive to psychedelic free spirit at a stroke.'

'I like my clothes bright, comfortable and warm, thank you,' said Faith, continuing to chop. 'Angela, my boss, doesn't. She's a lawyer, and she says neon pinks and greens are hard on her clients' eyeballs.'

'I don't doubt it. So you obliged her with the navy suit?'

'Of course,' she said airily. 'As well as a grey one and a black one.'

'Obliging *and* adaptable,' approved Max. 'How very——' He broke off abruptly. 'My God, what's that?'

'What's what?' Faith looked over her shoulder to see his finger pointed at the table. She followed its direction and said offhandedly, 'Oh, that's my special barbecued chicken.'

'I was afraid it might be. Why have you cremated it?' he demanded.

She smiled and turned back to the parsley. So Mr Know-it-All didn't know everything. 'I haven't,' she informed him smugly. 'That's black grape sauce.'

'Oh.' She heard him pull out a chair and sit down, heavily.

'What's the matter?' she began, swivelling around. 'Is something . . . ?' She stopped, swallowed her words, and wondered if her face had gone as chalk-white as it felt.

'Seen a ghost?' Max asked laconically. 'Don't worry, I think it's just your chicken.'

Faith brushed a hand across her eyes, but the view remained exactly the same, and she was uncomfortably aware that white had changed to pale pink. 'You,' she gasped. 'You—you're naked!'

'No, I'm not.' He was seated on the other side of the table and he stood up slowly.

Faith gasped again. No, he wasn't naked. Just the next thing to it. His skin gleamed bare and golden from his neck down to his waist, but a brief blue bathtowel was wound about his hips. Precariously wound, she noted, aghast. 'You—you can't come to supper dressed like that,' she managed to blurt. 'It's not—not decent.'

'It's perfectly decent. Didn't you tell me to use my imagination?'

'Yes, but I'd no idea it was so—so active.'

'Do you have a better suggestion?' The question sounded reasonable enough, but Faith had a feeling Max had no intention of sparing her maidenly blushes. In fact, she decided, he was greatly enjoying her embarrassment.

'Yes,' she said, regaining her presence of mind, 'I do have an alternative. Wait a minute.'

When she returned to the kitchen she was carrying a pair of faded jeans in one hand, and a paint-stained white shirt in the other. 'Try these,' she ordered.

Max put a hand to his jaw, and a mocking glitter lit up his eyes. 'I doubt if they'll fit,' he said mildly. 'You're not exactly my size.'

'They're not mine,' said Faith, not looking at him.

'Oh? Care to explain?'

'No.' She was damned if she was explaining to this condescending man that she had appropriated some of Stephen's cast-offs when she'd painted her old apartment in Seattle.

'Hmm.' Max's eyes narrowed, and he reached out to grab her wrist. Automatically she stepped sideways, because he looked very much as if he'd like to shake some kind of answer out of her, whether it was any of his business or not. But instead he dropped his hands, pushed himself unhurriedly to his feet, and accepted the clothes. As Faith watched him saunter out of the kitchen, all tanned flesh and supple movement, she couldn't contain a small, satisfied smile.

When he came back he was wearing the jeans and the shirt. They fitted him perfectly, as she had been quite certain they would.

'Your boyfriend and I take the same size,' he remarked, sitting down again and resting his forearms on the table. 'How convenient.'

'Ex-boyfriend,' said Faith, after a long pause during which she considered letting him believe she was spoken for. In the end she couldn't do it, because playing silly games wasn't her style.

'Ah.' Max leaned back in his chair looking complacent.

'But that doesn't mean I'm in the market for a new one,' she said quickly.

'I didn't suggest you were. Any more than I'm in the market for a girlfriend.'

'No, just a one-night stand,' said Faith, bristling. The moment the words left her mouth she regretted them.

With good reason. 'Is *that* an invitation?' he asked softly, bending forward like a cat about to pounce on a sparrow.

'No,' she said flatly. 'It's a joke. A very bad one.'

'Ah.' She watched him slowly exhale. Then after a brief silence he shrugged and asked carelessly, 'Have you sworn off men for good, then, Farraday, or just on a temporary basis?'

'I haven't sworn off men,' said Faith, wondering if she was wise to admit it, but annoyed by his patronising tone. 'Anyway, there aren't many unattached ones in Caley Cove.'

'So what's a charming young woman like you doing holed up in a small town in Washington with no men?'

'I didn't say there were *no* men. And as it happens I grew up in Caley Cove.'

'Never felt the urge to spread your wings? To investigate the big wide world out there?'

'Yes, of course I did.' She scraped parsley into a bowl. 'I left for college when I was eighteen, and after that I worked in Seattle. I came back to the Peninsula nine months ago after—after Stephen and I broke up. My family lives here.'

'Hmm. Came home to lick your wounds, did you?'

Faith whirled round, placed her palms flat on the table and glared down at him. Just as she had expected, a small smile was turning up the corners of his mouth. 'No,' she said tersely, her fine hair a swinging curtain across her face, 'I did not come home to lick my wounds. I came because my parents wanted me to, and because I figured I was ready for a change. I'll probably move again in a year or two.'

Max nodded. 'OK, I believe you. Thousands wouldn't.'

Faith took a deep breath and rolled her eyes up, resisting a childish urge to pull the wavy brown hair that curled so alluringly across his forehead. Obviously he didn't believe her. And he was right in a way. She had made up her mind to come home mostly because her two-year almost-engagement to Stephen had ended one warm July midnight.

Her vision blurred, and she remembered coming back to the apartment in Seattle after a pleasant evening out with friends. She had unlocked the door with no inkling of what was to come, and found Stephen in possession of her bed. He was sharing it with a leggy brunette whom Faith recognised as a new client of the law offices where both of them worked. A very wealthy client. Afterwards, she realised he had intended her to catch them. Stephen had always had a ruthless streak, and that was his way of letting her know the affair was over.

She remembered the first stunned moment of shock when she had thought inanely that this couldn't possibly be happening because she had never allowed Stephen to share her apartment and therefore he must be an illusion. But the key that lay on the bedside table was no illusion. She had given it to him.

Thinking back, Faith gave a little shudder. Even now, when she had recovered from the initial pain and devastation, and was getting her life back on track, it was hard to picture Stephen with another woman, to believe he was really gone from her life. Not that she wanted him back. She was over that. Somewhere in the future she might meet a man she could trust, but never again would she allow herself to be so gullible, to fall for a pretty face and a charming smile. Stephen had destroyed that naïveté in her, and, in a way, she knew she ought to be grateful for that.

For now, though, she was content to be alone.

'You're offended.' Her painful reminiscences were interrupted abruptly when Max lifted a hand and curved it round the back of her neck, holding her so that she couldn't move away.

'I'm not. Would you care if I was?' she asked, wishing she didn't like the feel of his firm fingers against her skin.

'As a matter of fact I would. But I don't believe I'd lose a lot of sleep over it.'

Faith frowned. 'Well, you haven't offended me,' she snapped at him. 'If you must know, I was more or less engaged to one of the partners in the law firm where I used to work. It ended, and yes, I *was* crushed. We'd been together for almost two years. And of course I couldn't stay in the office after that, so I had to give up my job as well. But in the end I was *glad* it was all over. At least I learned not to be so trusting.'

Max heard the slight break in her voice, saw too-recent pain in her lovely eyes, and felt an unexpected urge to rearrange a certain young lawyer's face. When he felt the muscles in Faith's long neck tighten, he let her go.

She straightened to push a lock of hair out of her eyes. 'I suppose we'd been drifting apart for some time,' she admitted, fixing her eyes firmly on a paint stain on his collar. 'Stephen always wanted everything his way. He thought he could mould me into his idea of the model marital partner. With himself in the senior position.'

'Quite a challenge,' murmured Max. 'Your ex was obviously an optimist.'

'No,' said Faith, wondering what had made her tell this stranger her private tragedy. 'He was an opportunist. And a jerk. Like someone else I could mention. I like to take life as it comes, Mr Kain, but that doesn't mean I'm a doormat.' She turned away and began to busy herself at the counter.

'Don't I know it.' Max spoke with feeling, but a moment later he was behind her, rubbing his thumb gently down the curve of her back.

She shook him off at once, picked up a potato and began to peel it as if she wanted it to fight back. 'Satisfied?' she asked bitingly.

'Not remotely,' Max replied, eyeing the tempting outline of her body through the soft fabric of her rainbow-coloured gown.

She made a sound in her throat that sounded to him like a snort, and went on peeling viciously.

By the time they sat down at the small white table to eat, Faith was in a thoroughly bad temper. She wasn't sure why, because by nature she was easygoing, but she knew it had everything to do with the sexy hunk seated across from her, and very little to do with the fact that she had peeled the potatoes with such grim dedication that there wasn't very much of them left.

'What,' Max asked lugubriously, 'is that?' He pointed at a small pink flower tucked beside the chicken on his plate, and he looked so glum that Faith began to perk up.

'It's a geranium,' she told him.

'So what's it doing on my plate?'

'It's edible,' she explained. 'You can eat it.'

'I don't want to eat it.'

'It won't hurt you. Snapdragons and lupins are toxic, but these scented-leaf geraniums have quite a pleasant and distinctive flavour.' She tilted her nose and nibbled daintily at a fragile pink petal.

'I don't want to eat lupins either,' growled Max.

'Didn't your mother ever teach you that it's not polite to complain about the food you're served when you eat in someone else's house?'

'My mother cooked mutton and mince and haggis. My mother did not cook lupins. She still doesn't.'

'Geraniums,' Faith corrected him, lifting a napkin hastily to her mouth.

'Same thing,' he muttered, taking a cautious bite of his chicken.

'You did invite yourself,' she pointed out.

The only answer she received was another growl, but after he had finished his mouthful he sat back, looking surprised. 'This black chicken isn't as bad as it might be,' he conceded.

'I'm flattered,' Faith said acidly. Then she hid a smile as she saw him push his geranium carefully under a decorative slice of orange.

Max finished the rest of his meal without further comment, and in more or less stoical silence. But when Faith got up to take a homemade apple pie out of the fridge she almost laughed outright at the look of glazed relief she saw in his eyes.

'I assume you're a fan of plain cooking,' she remarked drily. 'Meat and two veg and all that.'

'I'm a fan of practical cooking. In my business I don't have much choice.'

'What is your business?' asked Faith, seizing the chance to indulge her curiosity.

'Mountains,' said Max succinctly.

'Mountains?' She blinked. 'But you can't... You mean you make maps of them? Or run a ski lodge or something?'

'No,' said Max. 'I climb them.'

CHAPTER TWO

FAITH placed her fork carefully back on her plate. 'You climb them?' she repeated flatly. 'Mountains?'

'That's right.' Max was working his way through his pie with obvious relish.

'Oh.' She digested that. 'But—I mean, you can't make a living climbing mountains.'

'You most certainly can if you write best-selling books, take award-winning photographs and turn up sufficiently often on TV. The world's always had a fascination with mountains and the people who climb them.'

'Oh,' said Faith again. 'Yes, I suppose you can. If you're any good at it.'

Max's eyebrows lifted just a fraction. 'I'm very good at it,' he assured her. 'That's why I do it. Starving in a garret has never held the slightest appeal.' He finished the last mouthful, and hooked his arms loosely over the back of his chair.

Absentmindedly she shovelled another slice of pie on to his plate. Celebrity status in connection with this man hadn't occurred to her before. 'Where do you climb?' she asked doubtfully. 'Here in the Olympics?'

'Not normally, but since I was in the area anyway, I couldn't resist the chance to keep my hand in. Any new slope has to provide some sort of challenge.'

She nodded. 'Yes, there are lots of nice trails in the park. I've heard some of the climbs are quite easy, although this isn't the best time of year——'

'I don't usually do trails,' said Max.

There was something about his eyes that convinced Faith he had to be laughing at her. 'What *do* you do, then?' she asked, puzzled and a little annoyed.

'Alpine climbing, mostly. Unfortunately I managed to sprain my ankle on your Mount Constance, so I've been out of commission for a while.'

'Anyone climbing Constance in the winter deserves to sprain his ankle,' said Faith unsympathetically. 'Not that it looks sprained to me.'

'It isn't. I've been recuperating in Seattle with friends who've just left for Alaska.'

'Oh. Then why are you in Caley Cove now?'

'Is there some reason I shouldn't be?' Faith noted the slight flaring of his nostrils, and had a feeling she'd just been rebuked for cheeking her betters. Which Max wasn't.

'It's hardly a jet-set hot spot,' she said drily. 'I'd have expected you to choose somewhere more suited to your reputation.'

'And what do you know about my reputation?' He unhooked an arm from the chair to strum a reflective tattoo on the table.

'Nothing,' she admitted. 'I just thought——'

'That you saw the perfect opportunity to put me in my place. Which in your opinion *isn't* Caley Cove. Is that it?'

'Well...' Faith swallowed. He was altogether too close to the mark.

Max nodded as if she'd given him the answer he expected. 'I thought so. For your information, Miss Farraday, I have work to do. Notes to put in order for a book, and planning for an expedition I have in mind.

My friends suggested Caley Cove was an attractive small town where I could get on with what needs to be done without distraction.' He stopped abruptly and started strumming again. 'What do you think?'

Faith blinked, unnerved by the speculative way he was looking at her. 'I—I don't know. Why don't you go home to get your work done?'

'Home? I don't have a home. Unless you count my mother's house in Inverness.'

Oh, she thought. That explains the accent. Although it wasn't an accent really. It was the voice of a man who had travelled a lot and absorbed what he heard around him. An international sort of accent in a way. And obviously he wasn't married. She had wondered about that when he made his remark about not being in the market for a girlfriend.

'But surely you must have someone in your life,' she persisted, unable to believe that this maddening but very attractive man didn't have an adoring woman somewhere in his background.

He shook his head, and just for a moment his smoky eyes seemed to turn inwards, as if he were remembering something—or someone—he would rather forget.

'No,' he said. 'Contrary to your boringly female notion that every man needs a mate, I have absolutely no one in my life. Or no one permanent. What I do have is my freedom.'

So she was boringly female, was she? 'Freedom from what?' she asked tightly.

'To—not what.' He stared over her head, no longer appearing to see her. 'Freedom to climb mountains, to roam the world, to be my own man with no ties that bind to hold me at home. I'm not the rose-covered cottage type, Faith. My first and only love is climbing.'

He was serious now, not teasing, and she knew he meant what he said. He almost seemed to be issuing a warning, and, oddly, she felt as if she'd just lost something important—which was ridiculous.

'How interesting,' she said brightly, giving him her best brittle smile. 'So you've never cared seriously for anyone?'

Very briefly, his eyes turned darker. 'I thought I did once, years ago. Her name was Marilyn. But I soon learned that mountains and long-term love are incompatible.'

'How convenient,' said Faith, not able to hide her quite unjustifiable resentment.

He smiled frostily. 'Isn't it? So what do you think?'

'Think?' she echoed.

'Mmm. I'm leaving in a couple of weeks to do a series of programmes in Chicago. In the meantime, my friends were convinced this was one place where I wouldn't be able to get into too much trouble. I'm beginning to hope they were wrong.' There was a blatant question in his eyes that made Faith look quickly down at the table.

'They weren't wrong,' she said, in a voice which she hoped was incisive. Max Kain might be a man who avoided permanent ties, but obviously he wasn't averse to temporary diversions. She wasn't about to be one of them. 'Try getting into trouble here,' she informed him, 'and the whole town will be buzzing in half an hour.'

'Led by Mrs Gruber?'

She nodded. 'Yes, aided and abetted by Mrs Malone, Mrs Bracken, Mr Koniski——'

Max held up his hand. 'Whoa! I get it. You're letting me know, I suspect, and none too subtly, that if I'm thinking of taking you to bed I'd better do it somewhere other than Caley Cove.' He forked up a morsel of pie. 'Seattle has some interesting night life, but I prefer the country——'

'No,' said Faith, not batting an eyelid, 'I'm letting you know that Caley Cove hasn't much use for handsome rakes who think they're God's gift to women.'

'Ouch!' Max winced. Then he tipped his chair forward and laid two muscular arms on the table. 'So I'm a handsome rake, am I? How flattering. And what a delightfully old-fashioned phrase.'

'I'm an old-fashioned girl, Mr Kain.'

'Max.'

'Max. And if you're finished demolishing that pie, I think perhaps it's time you went home.'

'I told you I don't have a home.'

'I was thinking of the Clambake Hotel,' she said drily. 'Isn't that where you said you were staying?'

'Yes, but I don't think I want to leave yet. You haven't offered me coffee.'

'I don't drink coffee.'

'I might have known. Tea, then.'

'It's camomile,' said Faith with a small, faintly malicious smile.

Max groaned. 'My God, I feel like Peter Rabbit. Lupins *and* camomile tea.'

'Geraniums,' said Faith smugly. She stood up to fill the kettle.

When she turned round again, Max was on his feet too. He had his back to her and was staring through the window at the rain. Surreptitiously she ran her eyes over this pleasing example of masculine physique from behind. Really, if he weren't so damn sure of himself, Max Kain might be worth a woman's while.

'Nice view,' she remarked to his back.

He swung round at once, his full lips parted mockingly. 'I'm glad you enjoyed it.'

'Not *you*,' she snapped. 'I meant the view from the window.'

'There isn't one. You can't see the mountains through the rain.'

'Oh. Well, anyway...' Faith gulped. The view from the front wasn't unappealing either. Stephen's jeans fitted Max like skin, and the paint-stained shirt was missing several buttons. 'What—what mountains have you climbed?' she asked desperately. He could have climbed the moon for all she cared, but she had to say something to wipe that seductive leer off his face.

The leer grew more pronounced, as if he knew exactly what he was doing to her. 'You want a list?'

'No. No, just—just the main ones.' She licked her lips.

Max pulled his face into intimidatingly sober lines and began to tick off names on his fingers. 'Mount Cook, Mont Blanc, Annapurna, Everest——'

'Everest!' exclaimed Faith. 'What do you take me for, Max Kain? A complete idiot?'

'Sometimes,' he admitted.

'Well, I'm not, and you haven't climbed Everest.'

'You are on occasions. And I have.'

She put her hands on her hips, bunching her tent-like gown about her waist. 'How come I've never heard of you, then?'

'How many mountaineers *have* you heard of?'

'Well, there was Hillary. And Tenzing Norkay.' She stopped, unable to continue.

'My point exactly.'

Faith pulled out a chair and sat down. 'Have you really climbed Everest?'

'I've climbed a lot of mountains. It's what I do. Ever since I started rock-climbing as a boy in Scotland. And yes, I have climbed Everest. At the moment I'm between speaking tours and trying to scare up backing for another expedition to the Andes. Chicago's next on my schedule.'

He spoke with a matter-of-fact detachment that convinced Faith he was telling the truth. It explained those eyes of his too. Eyes that had seen places where humans were never meant to go. Eyes that had reflected fear and overcome it, had known the supreme elation of gazing out from the top of the world.

She wondered if Max had also achieved the profound contentment that must come from knowing you've done what you set out to do. As she had never done, because she had never been sure exactly what it was she wanted to do. Which, she supposed, linking her fingers in her lap, was why she had become a legal secretary after college instead of making use of her degree. Secretaries could change direction with much less soul-searching than academics.

She stared at Max now, silhouetted against the black, uncurtained window. He was no longer the annoying stranger who had disturbed her quiet time on the beach. He was a myth, a man of the ages, an explorer charting the unknown.

He was also incredibly sexy, and she would feel much less vulnerable once he left.

'I'm afraid camomile tea is all I have,' she said unsteadily, changing the subject. 'Since that obviously doesn't suit you, you'd better go.'

'The tea doesn't suit me,' he said softly. 'But Faith Farraday might.'

'I'm sure I wouldn't suit you at all.' Faith stood up stiffly. She felt at a disadvantage sitting down. And Max didn't seem like a myth any more, he seemed like Don Juan on the make.

'Why not let me be the judge of that?' His voice was still soft, and it curled around her senses in warm folds.

'Because I trust my own judgement better. I've just got over one oversexed, opportunistic male, and I'm not ready to take on another.'

Max had been half seated on the windowsill, smiling with the easy charm he seemed to assume without effort. But now his features tightened and closed up. Once again Faith was conscious of the strength of his jawline, and of the power contained in that taut, super-fit body.

'I don't believe I'm either oversexed or opportunistic,' he informed her coldly. 'If your Stephen was, I fail to see why you have any respect at all for your own judgement.'

Faith felt a slow burn begin to smoulder just below the surface of her skin. In a minute the smoke would be coming out of her eyes. 'And I,' she told him, 'fail to see why you bothered to intrude where you're not wanted, unless you were bent on taking advantage of what you perceived as an opportunity.'

'An opportunity to *what*?' he bit out.

'To—to take——'

'To take you to bed? Over Mrs Gruber's watchful ear? I thought we'd been over that already. No, Miss

Farraday, oversexed as I am, I assure you I had no plans to tumble you on to the carpet for dessert. The apple pie was quite adequate, thank you. And if a misguided appetite for home cooking led me to angle for an invitation to supper, then perhaps I am opportunistic. Experience has taught me the value of seizing promising conditions when they present themselves.'

'Well, you're not seizing me,' said Faith, still angry, but at the same time forced to admit, if only to herself, that perhaps she had jumped to conclusions.

'No,' agreed Max harshly. 'You've sure as hell got that right. I'm not in the habit of bedding witches.'

'I think you'd better leave,' said Faith, controlling her temper with difficulty. She wasn't sure why this man had the effect of turning her from a relatively placid, easy-going woman into someone who could fairly be labelled a witch. But it was certainly true that if Max wasn't out of this apartment in about two seconds she was likely to do something *he* would regret.

She, on the other hand, might feel considerably better.

'Your hospitality overwhelms me,' he said, still with that bite in his voice. 'But don't worry, I don't have any plans to spend the night.'

Faith turned her back on him and walked out into the living-room. 'You can keep the clothes,' she told him. 'I expect yours are still wet. Don't forget to take them with you.'

When he didn't answer she glanced over her shoulder and saw that Max had come into the room behind her. He was standing in the middle of the floor with his arms crossed, and there was a glitter in his eye that looked very much like the light of battle. She opened the front door quickly and stood holding it, while he continued to regard her with a speculative expression that made her take a quick step backwards. Which was odd, because she wasn't in the least frightened.

'Afraid I'm about to seize an opportunity?' he taunted, inaccurately interpreting her thoughts.

'No,' said Faith. 'I'm afraid you may refuse to go.'

'Why should I do that? The air-conditioning at the Clambake is warmer than the atmosphere in this room.' He swung away from her and disappeared into the bathroom. A moment later he was back, with his damp clothes hanging loosely over his arm.

'I'll get you a bag,' said Faith, smitten with an unexpected attack of conscience. He was right that she hadn't given him much of a welcome, and he was, after all, a visitor to town who hadn't really done her any harm. In fact he'd saved her from getting drenched in the downpour. Damp was a lot better than drowned.

'I don't need a bag,' he said curtly. 'Goodnight, and thank you for the black chicken.'

When he came to where she was standing, he stopped, and Faith held her breath as he stood quite still, staring down at her. She clutched the doorknob tightly, because his grey eyes made her think he was reviewing options which she wasn't prepared to consider. When he caught a lock of her hair in his free hand and tugged it gently, she gasped.

'Don't panic,' he said. 'I'm not going to kiss you.'

Before she could gather her wits to tell him that she hadn't been panicking because he certainly *wasn't* going to kiss her, he was already on his way down the stairs.

She walked across to the window and watched him cross the parking area to the Ford. It was still raining hard, and Stephen's shirt was plastered to his body in no time. Faith sighed. There was no getting away from it, Max Kain was a superb specimen of masculinity. He was also a most unusual man, with his knowledge of the classics and his love of mountains. But unusual or not, she was glad she wouldn't see him again.

'Very glad,' she said out loud, as she began to slam dishes into the sink with the kind of energy that she was well aware was likely to set Mrs Gruber to pounding on the ceiling with a broom.

'No banjo today?' asked Angela, raising her eyebrows as she watched her secretary prepare to leave the office carrying only a large black handbag.

Faith shook her head. 'No, I've decided to give it up for a few days.'

'Oh?' Angela pushed her pink glasses up her nose. 'What brought that on? An unexpected attack of the dismals? Or a commendable desire to behave like everyone else?'

Faith laughed. Angela always teased her about her tendency to do what she felt like doing whether her behaviour was conventional or not. But Caley Cove's only attorney knew quite well that Faith's nonconformity never extended to inconveniencing others. In the nine months since she had worked for Angela, replacing Sarah Malone, who had left to have a baby, the two women had formed a tolerant friendship.

'Neither,' replied Faith to her boss's question. 'There's a man in town I'd rather not run into.'

'Not your Stephen?'

'Oh, no. This one's a mountain climber who's just recovered from a sprained ankle. He's in between expeditions, he says.'

Angela pulled her glasses down her nose again and peered at Faith over the top of them. 'And why would a slightly damaged mountain climber be hanging about the beach in weather like this? There's a gale-force wind blowing out there.'

'I don't know, but he was yesterday,' said Faith simply.

'Good grief,' groaned Angela. 'You're two of a kind.'

Faith frowned. 'No, we're not,' she said, so emphatically that her employer's eyes narrowed. 'We're totally different.'

Angela nodded noncommittally. 'If you say so. Have a good evening.'

'Thanks.' Faith closed the door behind her and walked out into the street.

She also walked slap into a man who was standing on the pavement whistling. He had his hands in his pockets, and he appeared to be watching Harry Koniski lock the door of the real estate office across the road.

'Max!' she gasped, peeling herself off his powerful back and trying to subdue a pleasurable sensation in her stomach that had the effect of turning her complexion shocking pink. 'What are you doing here?'

'Waiting for you.' He turned round and regarded her flaming face with interest.

'Why? Last night you were comparing me to the air-conditioning at the Clambake—which, as you've probably already discovered, is always either arctic or off.'

'I compared the atmosphere in your *apartment* to the Clambake, which isn't the same thing at all. You, I stand a chance of warming up.'

'Oh, no, you don't.' Faith turned away. 'You shouldn't have wasted your time.'

'No waste. I'd nothing better to do.'

'Thanks.'

'Don't mention it.' He put his hand on her arm, and the wind blew her hair across his shoulder. 'Now, Miss Farraday, you may have the disposition of a witch, but you intrigue me. How about letting me repay you for the black chicken by taking you to the Clambake for dinner? Or is there some other restaurant in town?'

'Hal's Hamburgers,' said Faith.

'The Clambake it is, then.'

'Oh, no, it isn't. I'm not having dinner with you, Max.'

'Why not? Afraid I may succeed?'

'Succeed? At what?'

'Thawing the iceberg. Undoing the damage wrought by Stephen.'

'I don't want thawing. And Stephen didn't do any permanent damage—I wouldn't let him. What is it with you, Max? Can't you accept that I'm perfectly content with my own company?'

His grip on her arm tightened before he swung her around to face him and smiled down into her eyes. 'Sure I can. The point is, *I'm* not. There's not a lot to do around here, is there? And I don't see anything wrong with admitting that I'd enjoy the debatable pleasure of your company for a while. I'm no threat to your determined independence, Faith. I'll only be in town for two more weeks.'

Faith didn't tell him that was just the trouble. She had a feeling she could very easily fall for Maxwell Kain, and she wasn't really determinedly independent at all. She had intended to marry Stephen because she believed that two people who loved and cared for one another could form a partnership that was more fulfilling in every way

than any kind of militant individualism. But as she knew
to her cost, it was important to find the right partner.

Max wasn't that.

'I appreciate your interest,' she told him carefully, 'and
it's kind of you to ask me out to dinner, but——'

'But you're regretfully about to decline,' he said,
placing a finger under her chin and tilting it up. 'A pre-
vious engagement, I presume.'

'As a matter of fact, yes,' snapped Faith, twisting her
head away. 'If you must know, I'm having supper with
my family.'

'Hmm.' He looked at her as if he wasn't sure he believed her. But after a moment he took a deep breath
and said brusquely, 'I see. In that case I'll give you a
lift.'

'No need,' said Faith. 'It's not far.'

'I'll bet.'

Her eyes sparked. He thought she was lying. 'All
right,' she snapped, drawing herself up to her full height
but still not sure why his opinion mattered, 'you can
drive me there if you insist.'

'Thank you for your gracious permission,' he drawled.
'My car is just over there.'

'So I see,' said Faith, as he took her arm and hustled
her across the road. 'Is it really yours?'

'I didn't steal it,' he remarked drily.

'I don't mean that. But it doesn't look like you
somehow. I'd expect you to drive something fast and
sporty.'

'I drive whatever I can lay my hands on. It's rented,
of course.' The corner of his lip tipped up. 'Is that what
you think of me? Fast and sporty?'

She heard the quiver in his voice, noted the sensual line of his mouth, and said sharply, 'Fast anyway.'

'And you don't like speed?' The quiver was still there.

'No. Not in cars, and not in men either.'

'Ah. Thanks for the warning.' He opened the door of the Ford and helped her in.

Faith thought of half a dozen flattening responses, and immediately rejected them all. It wasn't worth sparring with this man. He would drop her off in less than five minutes, and that would be the end of that.

It wasn't, though. Because instead of dropping her off and driving away, Max parked the car in the driveway of her parents' single-storey white stucco house and climbed out to open her door.

Faith tried to ease her way past him without brushing against the soft grey sweater he was wearing over tapered grey trousers. But he moved and stood directly in front of her.

'Thank you,' she said formally, inclining her head, and hoping he'd get out of the way.

'My pleasure,' he replied, equally formal, but not moving. She noticed the wind lifting the hair on his neck.

'Faith?' The front door opened at that moment and Faith's mother appeared. 'Oh! Sorry, dear, I didn't know you had anyone with you.'

'I haven't,' said Faith, stepping on to the neatly cut grass and edging her way around Max. 'Be right with you.' As she started across the lawn she muttered out of the side of her mouth, '*Good evening*, Mr Kain. And thank you again for the ride.'

She didn't look round, but there was no sound of the car door slamming, and she knew he was still there, staring at her back.

'Who's the young man, dear?' asked Jane Farraday, patting her sleek white hair as Faith approached.

'He's just someone I met,' mumbled Faith. 'He gave me a lift.'

'Yes, I see that.' Jane raised her head and peered over her daughter's shoulder. After a brief pause, she called out to Max, 'Good evening. Won't you come in?'

Faith groaned inwardly. Her mother's matchmaking instincts had obviously kicked into high gear, which meant she approved of Max's looks. If she hadn't, she would have smiled vaguely and shut the door on him as if she hadn't even noticed he was there. Still, there was always hope. Max might do the right thing and decline.

But of course he didn't.

'Thank you, Mrs Farraday,' he said, his deep voice all warm appreciation. 'So long as I won't be intruding.'

Faith marched back across the lawn. 'Yes, you will be,' she said in a sibilant whisper.

'Did you say something?' Max asked levelly, but with a look in his eye that convinced her she'd lost the battle. 'Or do you have snakes in your garden?'

'Snakes?' Faith glanced down quickly. 'Not that I know of.'

'Oh, I thought I heard hissing. My mistake. I'm glad I won't be intruding.' He took her arm firmly and escorted her back to the house.

She suppressed an urge to stick out her high heel and trip him. He knew perfectly well that as far as she was concerned there would be one guest for supper too many. But there wasn't much she could do about it, because they were already standing on the steps being welcomed by a smugly smiling Jane.

Max, also smiling, but looking more purposeful than smug, put a hand in the small of Faith's back and moved her in front of him.

She stood stock-still, so he gave her a little shove and followed her into the home she'd grown up in.

To her own amazement, Faith managed not to stamp on his toes.

CHAPTER THREE

THE strains of 'Gloria, Gloria o Vincetori,' blared forth from the living-room as Faith and Max stepped across the threshold.

Faith grimaced. 'Still *Turandot*?' she murmured to her mother. 'Isn't Dad about ready for a change?'

Jane shook her head. 'Maybe in a week or two. You know your father.'

Faith nodded. 'I guess I do.'

Yes, she knew her father all right, and when he was in the throes of one of his obsessions nothing short of invasion from another galaxy was likely to distract him from the current fixation. For the last two months it had been opera, mostly *Turandot*.

'Where's Bruce?' asked Faith, who was trying to ignore Max's hand pressing her shoulder and not succeeding.

'Sound-proofing his bedroom,' said Jane. 'Your dad has decided the only way to shift him out of the house and into a job is by turning up the volume on his opera. It may work yet.'

Faith stifled a chuckle, and managed to shrug the hand off. Her young brother hadn't held a job since finishing high school, nor had he made the slightest effort to find one. Home suited him. He was fed, clothed, cleaned up after, and all at no cost to himself. Apparently her father had reached the end of his rope.

'Faith?'

Jolted out of her reverie, Faith saw that Jane was waiting for an introduction.

'Mother, this is Max Kain,' said Faith, in a voice that was as unenthusiastic as she could make it. 'Max, this is my mother.'

'I thought it might be.' Max smiled his slanted smile. 'Good evening, Mrs Farraday.'

Jane beamed, and Faith saw that with no effort at all Max had made a conquest.

'Won't you stay to supper?' her mother asked. 'You'll get tired of the Clambake food soon enough.'

Faith just managed not to gnash her teeth. 'I'm sure Max has other plans,' she muttered.

'You know perfectly well I haven't,' Max said evenly, and not bothering to lower his voice. 'I asked you out to dinner. Remember?' He spoke with a pleasant lightness, but she caught the underlying edge of reproof.

'Oh, yes, of course.' Faith tried to glare at him, but her mother was standing between them, looking brightly from one to the other, and the glare ended up as more of a manic grimace.

'So you'll stay,' said Jane. 'That's settled. Supper's not quite ready, but you can introduce Max to your father, Faith. And don't forget to get him a drink.'

Glumly Faith followed her mother across the hall towards the sound of Barbara Hendricks singing 'Signore, ascolta!'

'Frank!' shouted Jane Farraday. 'We have a guest. Turn that down.'

'Hmm?' Frank ran a hand over his short white beard, blinked vaguely, and reached for the controls of his stereo. *Turandot* became a background murmur, and

Faith introduced Max to her father as Jane, mission accomplished, departed for the sanctuary of her kitchen.

Max gestured at the much subdued stereo. 'That's an exceptionally fine recording of *Turandot*,' he said.

Frank's eyes lit up. 'You like opera?'

'I grew up on it. My parents played it incessantly on our ancient gramophone, and when I'm in the right city at the right time I always try to take in a performance.'

Faith smiled to herself at the look on her father's face. It was almost as if he were reciting a prayer of thanks to the Almighty for sending him a kindred spirit at last.

'Wonderful,' he said to Max, waving him into Jane's best rose velvet chair. 'My family are a bunch of philistines. Don't tell me my daughter is finally acquiring some sort of taste.'

'In music?' asked Max innocently.

Frank grinned. 'Maybe in music too. One can always hope.'

Faith raised her eyebrows and walked over to the mahogany drinks cabinet in the corner, leaving her father and Max to an enraptured discussion of the relative talents of Sutherland, Hendricks and Callas.

Half an hour later, the five of them sat down to supper. It began on a relaxed note. For once Bruce had brushed his long, tow-coloured hair, and for once Frank had nothing to criticise. Jane served the food with a pleased, social little smile, and Faith, recognising the signs all too well, suspected that Operation Son-In-Law was under way. Jane had never really liked Stephen, but she was of the old-fashioned persuasion that believed every woman needed a husband.

But at the end of the meal, when Jane and Faith came back from the kitchen bearing plates and two cherry cheesecakes, they saw the moment they entered the dining-room that the atmosphere at the table had changed.

Bruce was tugging at a yellow linen napkin, snapping the cloth as if he intended to rip it apart. Frank was sitting with his fists clenched on the table and his jaw thrust out like a blunt instrument. Max, leaning back in his chair, arms loosely crossed on his chest, appeared to be studying the pink-flowered frieze that decorated the top of the white walls.

Jane stopped dead, and nearly dropped one of the pies. Then, recovering herself, she moved to the table and set the dishes down as if she hadn't noticed anything amiss.

Faith stole a quick glance at Max and groaned inwardly. Having the family squabbles aired in front of comparative strangers wasn't something either she or her mother relished. But Jane was an optimist, and always hoped for the best. Faith had a more realistic turn of mind.

'I hope you like cherry cheesecake, Max,' said Jane brightly.

'Mmm.' Max withdrew his gaze from the frieze and glanced pointedly across the table at Faith. 'Love it.'

Faith pressed her lips firmly together and pretended not to see his white-toothed smile.

'Oh, good.' Jane eyed her husband anxiously. 'Frank, would you like some?'

Bruce snapped the napkin again, loudly, and Frank scowled. 'If I'm permitted,' he said grumpily. 'The professor of unemployment here seems to think I've no right to anything in my own house, unless it meets with his personal approval.'

'Oh, dear.' Jane handed Max a slice of cheesecake. 'Bruce, what have you done to upset your father now?'

'Everything I do upsets him,' muttered Bruce. 'All I did was ask if he had to talk about his stupid opera all evening.'

Help! thought Faith. This wasn't going to be any minor skirmish, this was shaping up to be a full-fledged family confrontation. Usually Bruce sat silent and surly throughout supper, while Frank needled him because he didn't know how else to handle his difficult son. But about once a month Bruce elected to fight back. Naturally today had to be the day.

She waited, holding her breath, for the next round. But to her amazement, before Frank could emit the anticipated roar of outrage, Max cut in smoothly.

'I was the one who introduced *La Traviata* into the conversation, Bruce. And I imagine your father was brought up, as I was, to display an interest in the interests of his guests. I'm sorry if the subject bored you.'

Iron and steel, thought Faith, trying not to gape. He's not sorry at all. He's putting Bruce firmly in his place—something, she had to admit, that her father had never quite managed to do.

Yet with just three succinct sentences, Max had reduced Bruce to red-faced apology.

'Sorry,' the young man muttered. 'I didn't mean—I mean, it's not that I was bored exactly. It's just that Dad——'

'Quite,' said Max, still steely. 'Perhaps you'd care to introduce a different topic?'

'Max climbs mountains,' said Faith, intervening before Bruce could suggest a discussion of his favourite rock bands, and before Frank, who she knew was only temporarily speechless, could reintroduce *La Traviata*.

Max glanced at her and delivered a slow, not very warm smile. 'And I thought you didn't care,' he murmured. 'How gratifying to find you remember.'

Faith frowned. He had a point, of course. She had been studiously ignoring him through most of the meal, for the very good reason that she didn't want to encourage his pursuit. 'You're not the sort of person one doesn't notice,' she said drily. 'As you very well know.'

Jane cleared her throat, making Faith jump guiltily. Her mother was right—she wasn't helping to diffuse an already fraught situation by taking snide sideswipes at Max.

She managed to produce a tight little smile. 'I mean you have the look of someone who's led an interesting life,' she explained, not altogether untruthfully. 'Why don't you tell us about it?'

'That's right, humour me,' he drawled.

'I'm not——'

'Do you really climb mountains?' Bruce interrupted.

'For my sins? Yes, I do.'

'Wow. Isn't it dangerous?'

'It can be. Less so if one uses caution and common sense.'

'Which you do, of course,' said Faith acidly. For some reason it irritated her to know that the element of danger was probably what had attracted Max to the slopes in the first place.

'I try to,' he said coolly. 'I've seen what can happen to careless climbers.'

'Like what?' asked Bruce, looking more animated than Faith had seen him in weeks.

That was all it took. After that, prompted by Frank, Max spoke quietly of risks that would have made most men quake in their boots—of avalanches and frostbite, of men pushed to the limits of endurance—and once, inadvertently, he betrayed that he wasn't as impervious to the ever-present possibility of disaster as Faith had assumed. That was when he spoke of a hazardous mountain rescue during which his good friend and partner had been swept to his death in a rock fall. Watching his face, Faith knew he hadn't meant to tell them about that. The pain still showed in his eyes, and in the way his knuckles tightened round his knife.

In spite of herself, Faith was impressed by his calm, unboastful delivery. It wasn't false modesty. He was proud of what he'd achieved and he saw no reason to hide it. But for all that, she had a sense that he was laughing at himself, that he knew only a crazy man would take the risks he took and turn them into a natural way of life.

And he would never change. She knew that too, with a certainty that surprised her. Any woman who wanted Max would have to accept the risks that loving him would inevitably bring. She glanced at him, sprawled easily in a chair, his body relaxed as it could never be on some icefield high above the rest of humanity...

She brought herself up with a start when she caught his grey gaze fixed on her in open speculation.

What was she thinking of? Why should she care what loving Max might mean?

'I'll get the coffee,' she said abruptly, jumping up and hurrying out to the kitchen.

Max watched her go, wondering what bee had stung this unpredictable woman now. For the life of him he couldn't remember ever being so attracted to a woman. Or so exasperated by one. She might not be a mountain, but she could certainly turn out to be a challenge ... He felt a faint stirring of anticipation.

Some time later, when it was time to leave, Max insisted on driving Faith home. It was impossible to refuse, because her entire family, even Bruce, was gathered round the door, gazing at him as if he were some kind of god.

'What did you do to them?' asked Faith, a little irritably, as she climbed into the car beside him. 'Do you dabble in black magic along with mountains?'

'I suppose it wouldn't occur to you that I might dabble in white magic?' he suggested caustically.

'Not for a moment,' she said. 'What *did* you do to them?'

'Nothing much. I offered to take Bruce rock-climbing, if that counts.'

'And he agreed?' Faith couldn't believe it. Bruce making an effort to haul his gangling body on to anything more taxing than a sofa was a prospect she found difficult to swallow.

'Indeed he did. As a matter of fact I had to dissuade him from setting out tonight.'

'Good grief.' Faith glanced sideways at Max's strong profile etched against the parking area lights, and wondered if he really was human. 'Nobody's been able to move Bruce further than the TV or the movies since he left school,' she said, shaking her head.

'Mmm.' Max fixed his eyes on the road. 'I imagine your brother is the sort of person who works in reverse. Push him one way, he'll go the other. But if something excites him it's a different matter.'

'It takes one to know one,' muttered Faith.

Max swung the wheel and pulled up in front of her apartment block. 'You, Miss Farraday, are beginning to get my goat,' he said warningly.

Faith tossed her head and started to get out, then paused as a thought struck her. 'You can't take Bruce climbing,' she said accusingly. 'You've sprained your ankle.'

He shrugged. 'It was a minor sprain. I've recovered.'

'Oh. Well, it's your ankle.' She frowned. 'I didn't know there *was* much rock-climbing round here.'

'There isn't.'

'Then I don't see——'

'There are, however, a few climbs Bruce could manage in the Needles area. Any more objections?'

'Of course not. It's just that——'

'It's just that you don't want me hanging around your family because it will make me that much harder to avoid. Is that your problem?'

Faith frowned, not liking the derisive tone of his voice. 'If you want to put it that way, then yes, that's my problem.' Unwisely, she turned to look up at him, and immediately wished she hadn't.

He was staring at her with an uncomfortably hard look in his eyes. The same look she had seen in the eyes of numerous adults during her childhood when she had followed her own inclinations and done something of which they didn't approve. In those days it had invariably been followed by retribution, and, glancing at Max now, she wasn't at all sure that pattern wouldn't be repeated.

But he only said evenly, 'What have I done to merit your animosity, Faith? Is my company totally repulsive? Have I threatened to beat you, or made a pass at you?'

'No. No, you haven't. Not seriously.'

'Then perhaps I should. That way you'd have genuine cause for complaint, and I'd have—a different kind of satisfaction.'

Faith gulped. 'What do you mean?'

He smiled, and it wasn't a smile that she cared for. 'When I first saw you, all I wanted was to find out what kind of crazy lady would play the banjo on the beach in a storm. Then, later, you asked me if I was satisfied. And I realised I wasn't.' His smile stretched, showing his teeth.

Faith reached quickly for the handle of the door.

Without haste, Max put his hands on her shoulders and twisted her about to face him. 'Not so fast,' he said softly. 'You want cause for complaint, don't you? I aim to oblige.'

Abruptly his palms slid off her shoulders and down her back. She gasped as strong fingers curved under her black skirt, lifting her towards him until one of her knees was trapped between his thighs, and the other was curled beneath the dashboard. Faith thought dizzily that she ought to struggle, but she had no strength, no will to move. She was enfolded in a haze of heat, a deep, explicit longing that could be sated only by this man with the tantalising hands.

Slowly his arms circled her waist, pulled her forward until her forehead was touching his lips. He kissed a small pulse in her temple, very lightly, and she lifted her head.

He kissed her again, on the mouth this time, gently at first, then harder as her lips parted. He slid his tongue in between her teeth. She gave a short, gulping moan and he tightened his hold. Then, before she realised what was happening, she was on her back, her head against the black fabric of the door, and Max was leaning over her, kissing her again, with a sensuous expertise that left her utterly vulnerable and disarmed.

She gave another moan and, to her total bewilderment, he sat up at once and said with devastating briskness, 'There, you see? I told you I'd give you cause for complaint.' When she couldn't find the breath to answer, he added with gravel in his voice, 'Or are you, perhaps, not complaining? If that's the case, I suggest we adjourn to your apartment. I'm not in the habit of making love to pretty women in cars.'

Faith struggled up while he sat motionless, watching her. 'You,' she said, finding her voice, 'are the most arrogant, self-satisfied man I've ever met. And that wasn't making love, that was juvenile, chauvinistic groping.'

'I quite agree with you,' he said. 'But it was the best I could do at short notice.'

'Oh!' exclaimed Faith. 'Oh! I don't believe you, Max Kain. You take advantage of my parents' hospitality, and then you take advantage of me, and—and you seem to think it's some sort of joke.' He did too, she realised. The light was on his face, and she could see his mouth. He was grinning like a devil looking for trouble.

'Not at all,' he said soberly. 'I thought it was very enjoyable. So, if I'm not mistaken, did you. And it certainly accomplished its purpose.'

'Purpose?' Faith spluttered.

'Mmm. I've provided you with *excellent* grounds for complaint, haven't I?'

She pushed at her dishevelled hair, made an effort to regain her control. This horrible, desperately attractive man was just paying her back. All that kiss had meant was that he was tired of her criticism and standoffishness and had come up with a pleasant way to chastise her. Pleasant for him anyway. And for her, if she were honest.

In fact it had been much too pleasant. Max Kain, with his love of danger and his lack of roots, was lethal. He was a man no woman would ever succeed in pinning down, and if one ever tried to she would be asking for all the heartbreak she would get. And she, Faith Farraday, was not a masochist. She was a normal young woman with normal, healthy needs which one day she would fulfil with a kind, reliable, ordinary sort of man who wanted the same things she did.

Max wasn't that man. But it was strange how *dull* reliable and kind suddenly seemed.

With a rising, and quite unreasonable, sense of panic, Faith grabbed the handle, wrestled open the door and almost fell out on to the concrete.

Max leaned across the seat and watched her as she scrambled to her feet. 'In a hurry?' he asked lazily.

'Yes,' she said, astounded to discover that for no particular reason she wanted to smile. 'In a hurry to get away from you.'

'Ah, of course. Time to fill out the complaint form.'

His deep laugh followed her all the way across the parking area until she slammed the door behind her to shut it out.

Mrs Gruber's door opened the moment she reached the second floor, but Faith hurried past her nosy neighbour with a muttered excuse about thinking her telephone was ringing.

It wasn't, of course.

After that, days passed without a single word from Max, and Faith almost began to wish the phone *would* ring. Contrarily, she missed the challenge of his provoking presence. Also, she had to admit, she missed his easy laughter and the sexy way his pale grey eyes glittered when they watched her cross the room.

On the third day, a Saturday, the phone rang the moment she got home from her weekly food shopping. But it wasn't Max.

It was her mother, the hysteria in her voice barely controlled. 'It's Bruce!' she cried. 'Faith, that man, Maxwell Kain—he took Bruce climbing two days ago. They were going to camp overnight. But they should have been back yesterday evening, and they're not. Your father's out with the Mountain Rescue. You—you don't think, do you, that there might have been an avalanche or something?'

CHAPTER FOUR

'No,' SAID Faith, gripping the phone, 'of course I don't think there might have been an avalanche. Not—not where they were going.'

In fact she had no very specific idea of where Max and her brother had been going. But Max was an experienced climber who ought to have known better than to encourage the semi-comatose Bruce to make such a radical departure from his normally somnambulent routine. Probably her brother hadn't been able to cope, so he'd fallen... She twisted the telephone cord tightly round her fingers and tugged it viciously. When Max came back she would tell him just exactly what she thought of him.

A soft mist formed in front of her eyes.

If Max came back.

Twenty minutes later, under a dark sky that threatened hours of heavy rain, Faith hurried up the path of her parents' house to be met by her mother at the door.

'Any news?' she asked, knowing from Jane's face that there wasn't.

Jane started to shake her head, then Faith's eyes widened as she saw her mother freeze, with her mouth hanging open like a trout. Her stunned gaze was fixed on the road.

Faith turned round. At the top of the short street, a silver-grey Ford had just swung round the corner. It was covered in mud and the left side was badly dented, but the man behind the wheel was obviously well in control, and, as the car pulled up, they could see that the passenger beside him was also in possession of all his body parts. Bruce looked tired, bedraggled and a bit stiff, but more contented than Faith had seen him in months.

Jane was already in the driveway, tugging at the door of the car.

'What happened?' she demanded. 'Bruce, are you all right?'

'Sure I am.' Bruce looked surprised. 'Why? You weren't worried, were you?'

'Now why would she be worried?' scoffed Faith, coming up behind her mother. 'You're only sixteen hours late, the weather's awful, and you've never climbed a rock in your life, much less a bit of a mountain.' When Bruce only gaped at her, she turned her glare on Max, who was easing himself out of the car. 'As for you,' she said, 'you ought to be ashamed of yourself. Scaring my mother half to death and not even having the decency to phone.'

Max stared at her, his eyes narrowing. 'I tried to phone,' he said curtly. 'Your mother's line was busy each time I called.'

Jane put a hand to her mouth. 'I'm afraid it could have been,' she admitted. 'I phoned Molly Bracken several times, and Clara Malone. I didn't want to worry *you*, Faith. And I felt I had to...'

'Yes, of course,' said Faith hastily. It figured, she thought. Even in an emergency, it was entirely in keeping for her mother to tie up the phone.

She turned back to Max.

'So what was wrong with calling last night?' she demanded.

'Not much,' he replied. 'Except that we were miles from a phone.'

'Well, you shouldn't have been. You told Mother you'd be home yesterday evening.'

'Faith, it wasn't Max's fault,' Bruce began.

'It's all right, Bruce.' Max held up his hand. 'I'll deal with your sister. In the meantime, I suggest you explain it all to your mother and give her a chance to count your fingers and toes.' He smiled at Jane. 'I'm sorry you were worried, Mrs Farraday. We tried to get in touch the moment we could.'

'Yes, yes, I'm sure you did.' Jane's anxious gaze strayed to her mud-stained son. 'Never mind, now that I can see you're both fine...' She took Bruce's arm. 'Come along. You could do with a bath, among other things.'

'Hold on a moment,' said Bruce. 'Max——'

'I'll be in touch.' Max raised a hand to the young man. 'Right now your mother wants you to herself. Faith, I'll take you home.'

'In that mud-trap?' scoffed Faith, resenting his peremptory tone. 'I'd sooner walk, thanks.'

'Suit yourself.' Instead of demanding compliance, as she'd half expected, Max climbed into the car and watched while she said goodbye to her mother and brother. Ignoring him, Faith marched down the driveway with her head up. But when she turned into the road, he was beside her, matching the speed of the Ford's engine to her walk.

'I don't need an escort,' she snapped.

'Maybe not, but it amuses me to watch you play the Duchess—you do it so well. Especially with the wind blowing your hair into a bird's nest, and your nose turning blue with the cold.'

Faith clamped her lips together and didn't answer. She wouldn't give him the satisfaction. Besides, if she opened her mouth she was sure she would either burst into tears at the sheer relief of knowing Bruce was safe—or, and she hated to admit it, burst out laughing in response to the outrageous provocation in Max's eyes.

She completed the short walk home in what she hoped was a regal silence, and refused to look at him again. But he stayed right beside her, the throb of the engine not quite drowning out the wind. She was sure that, if she made the mistake of glancing at his face, she would find that he was laughing at her again.

The most infuriating aspect of the whole situation was that she didn't think she could altogether blame him. She probably *was* making an idiot of herself.

All the same, she was not getting into his car. She'd made that mistake once too often, and Max was *not* the kind of man she wanted to become involved with.

By the time she reached her apartment block she was shivering, and the rain had begun to pelt down in earnest.

Max pulled the Ford to a deliberate stop just in front of her, and she quickened her pace to get around him.

She might as well have saved herself the effort, because she no sooner had the key in the lock than he was beside her, his hand on her elbow and his breath warm and caressing on her neck.

'Go away,' said Faith.

'Why?'

'Because—because I don't want company.'

'Especially mine.' His voice didn't sound warm and caressing after all. It sounded cold.

'That's right. After your performance the other night, what else can you possibly expect?'

'My performance wasn't up to par, I admit. I can do better.'

'You're not getting the chance.' She pushed open the door and tried to slam it in his face, but he was too quick for her, and too strong. The next moment he was in the hall beside her.

Faith took a deep breath. 'Max, I said I didn't want company.'

'I know. But I do. I'd also like to tell you why we were sixteen hours late getting back.'

She eyed him warily, curiosity vying with indignation. 'All right, I'll give you five minutes. But if I let you in, do you promise to leave quietly as soon as you've told me what happened?'

'I'm already in,' he pointed out. 'I don't have to promise you anything.'

'You're not in my apartment. And if you don't promise I'll—I'll call Mrs Gruber.'

To her annoyance, Max let out a shout of laughter. 'Faced with a threat like that, what can I do?' He gave an exaggerated shrug. 'All right, Duchess, I promise.'

Not without misgivings, Faith took him at his word and started to climb the stairs to her apartment.

'OK,' she said, as soon as they were safely inside, 'so tell me what happened.'

'Aren't you going to ask me to sit—or should I say lie—down?'

'You're covered in dirt.'

'And you're all wet. We'd make wonderful mud pies together.'

'We're not making anything together, Max Kain.'

'I was afraid we weren't. How about a bath, then? Separate ones,' he added, grinning, when he saw her eyes flash.

Faith frowned at him. He needed a bath. His jacket was clean, but the shirt underneath was streaked with mud. So were his khaki trousers. There was a smudge of dirt on his cheekbone, and she had no doubt that his forearms were also in need of soap and water. But she had no more clothes to offer him, and there was no way she was holding a conversation with Max while he lounged about on her cushions modelling a towel. She'd been that route once already.

'No,' she said. 'You can have a shower at the Clambake. Just say what you want to say, and go.'

His eyes narrowed, and the look he gave her made her feel cold inside. She was already cold on the outside.

'What I have to say,' he said, 'is that, after an easy climb at which your brother did remarkably well for a beginner, we ran into a bit of a problem——'

'Through no fault of your own, I suppose.'

'You suppose right. And don't be sarcastic.' He crossed his arms on his chest, and Faith wondered why he always looked so much taller than he actually was.

'I wasn't——'

'Yes, you were. As I've been trying to tell you, we ran into a problem, on our way home. We'd been on a back road without seeing a soul for some time when this truck full of kids came roaring round a corner on the wrong side, and ran smack into us. They'd been drinking. All of us ended up in the ditch, which still had a few inches of snow. Lucky for us, because there was a fairly steep drop on the other side.'

Faith blanched, as a nightmare of blood and twisted bodies blurred her vision. What if Bruce—or Max...? She forced herself back to the reality of Max's perfectly healthy presence in her apartment. 'You—they—was anyone hurt?' she asked, biting her lip.

'Not terminally. The gang in the truck took one look at the damage and passed out. So we piled them into our tent, spent the night by the side of the road, and managed to right the car in the morning. As far as I know the truck's still there. I took the kids home with well-deserved headaches and bruises, and immediately tried to call your mother.'

'You can't have tried very hard. She wasn't on the phone *all* day.'

'Look,' said Max grimly, curling a muddied hand round her upper arm, 'your brother had just had the kind of night I'd say he's not one bit used to. He survived very well, and he was more help than the rest of them put together when it came to righting the car. But he was cold, exhausted and stiff, and I figured he'd had enough. The important thing had to be to get him home, and if your mother was chatting on the phone each time I called her—four times, for your information—it didn't seem to me she was that worried. In fact Bruce was convinced your parents would appreciate the time to themselves.'

'He would be,' said Faith.

Max put his free hand round her other arm. 'Don't underestimate Bruce,' he said curtly. 'That's probably been half his problem. If enough people tell you you're a lazy, incompetent drone, then that's exactly what you become.'

'Oh, sure. And I suppose *you're* an expert on family relations,' taunted Faith.

'No, but I've damn well had to learn to get along with people. To work as part of a team for the success of an expedition. If you give someone a job to do, expect them to do it, and don't wait around for excuses, nine times out of ten it will get done.'

Faith tried to step back, but he was still holding her. She was conscious of his nearness, of the earthy, male scent of him, and the probability of mud on her grey suit. She could live with the mud, but she didn't think she could tolerate Max's overpowering presence much longer. He was arousing all sorts of feelings in her that she didn't want aroused. Desire, certainly, there was no point in denying it. But there was more to it than that. She wanted Max, but she also wanted him to leave. He made her feel inhospitable and ungrateful and guilty, and because she was usually none of those things she didn't like the feeling at all. If he left, she'd be comfortable again.

'You may be right about Bruce,' she said coolly. 'Perhaps you should take it up with my parents. Incidentally, is that why you insisted on coming in? To talk about Bruce?'

'No. I insisted on coming in because I misguidedly fancied your company.' He released her arms and chucked her under the chin. 'I should have known better, but when I want something enough I'm a slow learner.'

'Want something?' she gulped, mesmerised by the lazy smoke in his eyes.

'Mmm—you. I want to see what's under that touch-me-not suit of yours, I want to smooth my hands over that soft, country-cream skin——'

'Stop it,' said Faith desperately, running her tongue over lips that were suddenly dry. 'That's not funny, Max. You said you'd leave quietly——'

'But I am leaving—very quietly. Goodbye, Faith.'

She closed her eyes, and only opened them again when she heard the door close. Very quietly, just as he had said.

But long after he had gone she remembered the way he'd looked as he turned away—distant, a little angry, as if he wanted something but didn't quite know what it was. He had said he wanted her. But it was more than that, she was sure of it. Or was she imagining things? Did Max just expect to return when it suited him, and scoop her into his bed?

If he did he had another think coming, because the one thing she had learned from Stephen was to be wary of attractive men on the make. Especially the love-'em-and-leave-'em type, which Max had frankly admitted he was.

She could do without that kind of union.

For the next few days Faith heard and saw nothing of Max, and again she was surprised to find how much she missed his aggravating presence in her life.

She knew now that she was over Stephen. Funny, a week ago she hadn't been sure, but now the thought of her ex-fiancé brought only a fleeting pang of mortification at her own gullibility in being duped by so shallow a man. Only, if the time had come for her to take a renewed interest in the opposite sex, why, oh, why had that interest been sparked by Max Kain, who was more honest than Stephen, certainly, but about as temporary as the balance in her bank book?

Faith was alone on her favourite bit of beach when that thought came to her, and at once she plumped herself down on her log and began to strum desultorily on her banjo. Of course, the fact of the matter was that she wasn't all that interested in Max. She was merely suffering from a case of spring hormones.

'And whoever invented hormones has a lot to answer for,' she muttered to a small passing crab.

The crab scuttled under a rock.

Faith rubbed the sleep from her eyes and pushed herself up on her pillows. What in heaven's name was happening? Why did her quiet apartment, early on a Wednesday morning, sound like a construction site working on a deadline?

She realised her alarm was ringing, and turned it off. The noise didn't stop. Oh! Her phone was ringing too. And Mrs Gruber was caterwauling downstairs. But most of the racket was caused by a fire truck shrieking down the street outside her window.

She stumbled into the living-room and grabbed the phone from beneath a precarious pile of orange cushions. The pile collapsed on to the floor.

'Faith?' It was her mother calling. 'Faith, have you heard the news?'

'No,' said Faith. 'I've heard my alarm, the telephone, Mrs Gruber and a fire engine, but not the news.'

'But that *is* the news. The Clambake Hotel's on fire!'

Trust her mother, thought Faith. By now Jane Farraday probably knew exactly what had caused the blaze as well. 'What...?' she began. Then she stopped, as something clammy and frightening seemed to ripple like wind across her heart.

Max was staying at the Clambake.

'Has anyone been hurt?' she asked quickly. 'Have you heard?'

'No, but Molly Bracken and Clara Malone are on their way down there. They're going to call me.'

Of course, thought Faith morosely. All of Caley Cove will be on its way down there by now, and the fire department won't be able to get through.

She looked at the clock. Fire or no fire, Angela would expect her at work.

Her mind on the people—one person in particular—who might be trapped or injured at the hotel, Faith grabbed the first thing she could find from her cupboard. It was a loose, meadow-green dress with scarlet poppies embroidered around the hem and neckline.

When she went outside after a hasty breakfast of toast, she discovered that the air was thick with smoke. Without thinking, moving like a robot responding to its master, she turned in the direction of the fire.

The Clambake was in the centre of town surrounded by offices and shops, and by the time Faith got there it seemed as if every inhabitant of Caley Cove, along with half the population of the surrounding countryside, had gathered to take part in the drama. But contrary to Faith's expectations, the fire truck was parked reassuringly by the kerb.

She had imagined there would be flames soaring to the sky, but, although a pall of smoke hung over the stricken building, only a few pale tongues of fire still licked stealthily at one end of a new wing built close to the road. Two firemen were hosing the scorched walls, and the air, which was flecked with cinders, made her choke. But the main part of the green and brown chalet-style building seemed to have escaped major damage. The blaze had not spread to the nearby shops.

Which part of the hotel had Max been staying in? She looked around her, searching for someone who might know, and her gaze fell on Jane's friend Molly Bracken. Molly always knew everything. Faith hurried up to touch her on the arm.

'Mrs Bracken, are all the guests safe?' she asked, trying hard to control the quiver in her voice.

'I think so,' said Molly, bright eyes wide with excitement. 'But everyone's talking about some visitor who rescued Nate Spellman and his wife. I arrived too late to see it, sad to say.' Her voice was heavy with the disappointment of glorious opportunity missed.

'Nate Spellman?' repeated Faith dazedly.

'Yes—you know, the insurance man. He comes through about four times a year.'

Faith didn't know, but she wasn't surprised that Molly did. 'The man who rescued them,' she murmured, taking a deep breath, 'who was he?'

'I haven't been able to find out. Oh, look.' Molly pointed across the road. 'That must be him. They're taking him to the ambulance now.'

'Ambulance?' whispered Faith. She hadn't noticed the white van parked beside the kerb.

'Yes—I heard he smelled smoke and broke the door down. Gave the alarm too. Nate and his wife were asleep, but he got them out. Looks like one of them was smoking in bed.'

'But they weren't hurt?'

'I don't think so. The cigarette fell on the rug, not the bed, and that man moved fast. Then he went back in, the damned fool.'

Faith closed her eyes. She didn't know for sure that the man was Max, but if anyone was going to be that sort of damned fool it was probably him.

'Why did he go back?' she whispered.

'Thought there might be someone else in there—a kid, I guess. But he's still alive. At least, that's what Jerry from the Fire Department said.'

Thank God! thought Faith, peering across the street at the stretcher being carried across the sidewalk. She tried to see if she could recognise the body. When she couldn't, she took a step forward, but was halted by the long arm of the law.

'Sorry, Faith,' said Constable Smith, shaking his head importantly. 'Have to ask you to keep out of the way. Got to get the ambulance through.'

'Yes,' said Faith. 'Yes, of course. Who—do you know who he is? The man on the stretcher?'

'Nope. Guest at the Clambake, I'm told.'

The ambulance took off down the street. Faith stared after it, and at that moment the clock on the Town Hall started to strike. Eight-thirty. She was late for work. And even if the injured man *was* Max, there was nothing she could do for him now.

With a murmured goodbye to Molly, she hurried down the street towards her office.

'My God!' groaned Angela, the moment she came through the door.

'What's the matter?' Faith stared at her blankly.

'That—that grass-coloured nightmare with the poppies. You'll scare the clients.'

'Oh,' said Faith. 'Sorry.' She glanced down at her meadow-green frock. 'I wasn't thinking. Mother phoned about the fire, and——'

'Ah,' Angela took her glasses off, 'of course. Maxwell Kain, the hero of the hour. I might have known.' She sighed. 'Not long ago I had Sarah Malone looking like a ragbag because she'd fallen in love with Brett Jackson. And now I have you, looking like Flanders Fields, presumably because of your Max. Thank God I had the sense to get divorced. Oh, and don't worry, I've heard your man's going to be just fine, though he may have suffered a bit of smoke inhalation. They're keeping him in hospital for observation. According to reliable sources, he collapsed just outside the door of the hotel. But he'll be all right.' As Faith started to head for the door, she added, 'And no, you can't have the morning off. No visitors until this evening—I checked.'

'Oh. Oh, thanks.' In a daze Faith wandered back to her office, peeled off her jacket and sat down.

For the rest of the day she carried on with her work like an automaton, taking in little of what was happening around her. All she could think of was that the man who had been the bane of her life for the past week was in hospital. And he had risked his life for two people he didn't even know. Somehow that didn't surprise her. But she felt a great need to go to him, to tell him that, thanks to his influence, Bruce had decided to take a mineralogy course. That she was grateful for his help, sorry if she'd misjudged him, and maybe...

No, she wouldn't take that thought any further.

At seven o'clock, still wearing the meadow-green dress, Faith was hurrying down the hospital corridor. Room 112, Myrtle at the desk had told her.

At first, when Faith looked into the private room, she thought for a second that the lump in the bed had no head. Then it moved, and a mane of springy brown hair appeared from under a blanket as Max rolled over to inspect his visitor. After a moment he put a hand over his eyes.

'Ouch,' he said. 'Is that garment meant to resurrect the remains? Or are you hoping to lay me out for good?'

'What remains?' asked Faith. 'You look remarkably mortal to me.'

It was the truth. With the blanket now pushed down almost to his waist, his hospital gown impatiently discarded, and his legs forming a sturdy shape beneath the blankets, he looked entirely male, disturbingly seductive and—oh, yes—very much alive. Especially his eyes, which seemed to be engaged in undressing her.

'Mmm,' he said pensively, 'I think I *could* be persuaded to rise from my deathbed. Or better still, perhaps you could be persuaded to join me.'

Faith frowned. 'You're a complete fraud, aren't you?' she said, setting her bag down on a chair. 'What is this, some fancy new line of seduction? Pathetic wounded hero on last gasp—can only be resurrected by health-giving injection of sex?'

'What a splendid idea,' said Max. 'Now why didn't I think of that myself?'

Before she realised what was happening, he had grabbed her wrists and pulled her down on top of him.

'Oh!' she gasped, squirming and trying to stand up. 'Max, what do you think you're doing? This is a hospital, you're supposed to be recovering——'

'Keep that up and I may recover fast,' he growled huskily into her ear. His hands held her wrists at her sides, and she stopped squirming abruptly as she felt his arousal right through the thickness of the blanket.

'Really, Mr Kain! I'm sorry, but this isn't the place...'

Max released her with unflattering speed as the voice of officialdom rang out from the doorway. She slid her feet to the floor and turned, red-faced, to meet the disapproving stare of Nurse Nellie McNaughton.

'Hello, Nellie,' she mumbled. 'I wasn't—this wasn't—I mean, I slipped, and just happened to fall on the bed...' She let the words trail off as she saw that Nurse McNaughton didn't believe one word of it.

'Of course,' said the nurse, poker-faced. 'All the same, Mr Kain is supposed to be recuperating——'

'I've recuperated,' said Max, grinning at her. 'The doctor says you're throwing me out in the morning.'

'Oh, not *throwing* you out, Mr Kain. We're all very grateful for what you did, but——'

'But you need the bed, and there's nothing the matter with me,' Max interrupted her. 'I can't argue with that.'

Nurse McNaughton smiled cautiously and, after a reproving look at Faith, tossed her red hair and left the room.

'I suppose you think that was funny,' said Faith, putting several feet between herself and the bed.

'Amusing, certainly,' he agreed.

Faith lifted her chin. 'Not that it matters,' she said, assuming an air of indifference. 'Because of course you'll be moving on now that the Clambake's closed for repairs.'

'Will I?' Max smiled enigmatically.

'Well, what else can you do?'

'Any suggestions?' His rich, molasses-warm voice stroked softly over her sense of self-preservation, and the look in his eyes started doing impossible things to her reason.

'I—don't you want to leave Caley Cove?' she asked, stalling, and knowing it was the wrong thing to ask.

'Eventually, yes. But not just yet. There's something I'd like to do first.'

'And what's that?'

He shrugged his naked shoulders against the pillow and gave her a tip-tilted smile. 'You figure it out.'

Faith sighed. The challenge was in his eyes again, and she had a feeling she didn't need to figure it out. The desire to apologise for misjudging him faded fast. But there was something utterly seductive and hypnotic about the man lying before her on the bed. She didn't want him to leave. She wished she did, but she didn't. And she owed him something, for Bruce's sake if for no other reason ...

'If you like,' she said, the words dragging out of her like weights, 'you could stay with me for a few days. If you don't mind sleeping on a pile of cushions. I'm not giving up my bedroom.'

'Did I ask you to?' Max's grey eyes gleamed a smoky insinuation.

Faith gulped, and he sat up suddenly and laughed. 'Don't worry, Duchess, I won't attempt to cross your maidenly portals unless I'm asked. And I have no particular prejudice against cushions.'

Faith tried her best to look repressive and at the same time quell a quick curl of excitement in her stomach. 'There's no danger of your being asked to cross anything,' she assured him, 'but if you don't mind the cushions, and if you'd like to stay——'

'Yes,' said Max, his mouth curving so seductively that Faith caught her breath. 'Yes, Duchess, I think I would like—very much. Shall we seal the bargain in the usual way?'

He held out his hand.

CHAPTER FIVE

FAITH took a quick step backwards. 'That won't be necessary.'

'Perhaps not.' Max smiled lazily. 'I was thinking more in terms of inclination than necessity.'

'No,' said Faith again, wishing her voice didn't sound hoarse.

'What's the matter, Duchess?' His eyebrows rose annoyingly. 'You're as safe as a nun with the dragon nurse patrolling the halls.'

'Maybe,' said Faith. 'But there are other pitfalls.'

'Pitfalls?' exclaimed Max. 'Is that what you think I am? A pitfall?'

She wrinkled her nose. 'Yes,' she replied succinctly, lowering her head to grope around in her bag. 'Here, take the spare key to my apartment.' She threw it at him, and he caught it. 'I'll be at work by the time they let you out tomorrow, so help yourself to anything you need.'

'Now what man could resist an invitation like that?'

Max's smile was so suggestive that Faith turned away, not wanting him to see her blush. What on earth had she let herself in for, with her impulsive invitation to this totally impossible man? Or had it been only an impulse? Was she, in fact, going deliberately out of her mind?

'I meant,' she said firmly, 'that you could help yourself to food and drink. And to towels—things like that.'

'But not to the hostess.' Max heaved an exaggerated sigh. 'I thought it was too good to be true.'

Faith refused to let him provoke her. She was going to keep on top of this situation if it killed her. 'I'll see you tomorrow,' she said briskly over her shoulder. 'Have a good night—pitfall.'

As she hurried down the hall past Nurse McNaughton and a group of curious aides, she heard Max's voice shouting after her, 'Who the hell do you think you're calling a pitfall, Duchess? I'll have you know...'

She didn't hear what he'd have her know, because she covered her ears.

It wasn't until she reached the revolving doors to the parking area that she realised she'd have to return to the lion's lair. In her hurry to leave, she had forgotten to pick up her bag.

She scudded to the door of Room 112 intending to grab her missing property and leave as quickly as she could. But just as she reached the threshold she heard a giggle, followed by a man's low chuckle. She paused for a moment, swallowed, then took a quick step forward.

Nurse Nellie was standing beside the bed wearing the most idiotic smile Faith had ever seen. It reminded her of a dog's wriggling gratitude for a casual scratch behind the ear. Max was holding her hand and laughing up into her face.

'Really, Mr Kain,' giggled Nellie, 'you shouldn't say things like that!'

'Has he been telling you you remind him of Euterpe?' asked Faith coldly, as she marched into the room and seized her bag. 'Or Eir, perhaps? She's the goddess of healing, I believe.'

Nellie withdrew her hand as if it had been scorched, but Max only laughed and said, 'Bullseye! How did you guess?'

'It wasn't hard,' said Faith, who was seething with a resentment she knew she had no right to feel.

'It worked too, didn't it, Nellie? You stopped scowling at me.' Max was not at all repentant. 'Ah, now don't start again. You're a whole lot prettier when you smile.'

Nellie, obviously a little out of her depth, ventured a half-hearted grin and scurried out, mumbling about an ulcer in Room 222.

'I hope you're pleased with yourself, Max Kain,' said Faith disgustedly. 'That wasn't fair. Nellie's going steady with Ted Koniski.'

'What wasn't fair? Making her smile? It's a great improvement. Did her the world of good too.'

'Did you the world of good, you mean. Couldn't resist the opportunity to make a conquest, could you?'

'Very easily,' he said, no longer laughing. 'Nellie needed cheering up. She's having trouble with young Mr Koniski.'

'Oh, and of course you're just the one to help her out.'

'Jealous?' he asked. There was a curious harshness to his voice now that didn't quite fit the taunting question.

'Of course not. Why should I be jealous of Nellie?' Faith lifted her chin, and when she felt heat begin to flow into her cheeks she turned away and hurried out of the room.

Behind her she thought she heard him laugh, very softly.

'Damn you, Maxwell Kain,' she muttered under her breath. 'Do you have to be such a jerk?' And why had she been fool enough to give him her keys and invite him into her home? It was probably the dumbest thing she'd done since she allowed herself to fall in love with Stephen.

Love, she thought contemptuously. It was supposed to make the world go round, but all it really did was turn women into starry-eyed idiots—and men into predatory beasts.

She shoved at the revolving door and stubbed her toe hard on its brass edge.

Her arms laden with groceries, Faith paused in the parking area when she arrived home the following evening. She didn't see Max's car, but there was a beige Ford she hadn't noticed before, so perhaps he'd replaced the dented silver-grey. Or perhaps, with luck, he hadn't come.

By the time she reached the third floor she was breathing rapidly, and not entirely because the groceries were heavy. She hesitated, then opened the door, closing it quietly behind her.

Max was lying on a bank of blue cushions. His hands were behind his head, and at first Faith thought he was sleeping. She put the bags on the floor and allowed her gaze to stray with reluctant appreciation over his tough, muscular body. Mmm, very nice. Firm in all the right places. Well-built, without a single ounce of extra fat. And with that brown T-shirt stretched across his chest, and the form-fitting beige jeans which he hadn't bothered to fasten... She moistened her lips as her eyes took in the wide leather belt tossed carelessly on the carpet beside him.

'Like what you see?' he asked lazily.

Faith jumped, and saw that he wasn't asleep after all. In fact he was awake and studying her from under heavy lids in much the same way that she had been studying him.

'You'll pass,' she said. When he smiled complacently and held out his arms, she added dampingly, 'In the dusk with the light behind you.'

'Why, you little...' Max sat up, scattering cushions in all directions, and Faith backed away as he rose lithely on to his feet—without bothering to fasten his jeans.

'What do you think you're doing?' she demanded as he advanced towards her.

'I'm about to become a pitfall,' he told her, 'in daylight with the light in front of me.'

She took another step backwards and ended up pressed against the door.

'Now,' said Max softly, placing his palms flat against the pale cream wood beside her head, 'I've got you where I want you, haven't I, Duchess?'

Faith held her breath. 'No, you haven't. You promised,' she managed to gasp. His closeness and the crooked lift of his mouth were having their usual fatal effect.

'Not to help myself to my hostess?' His voice was smooth and silky. 'True, but that was before I caught her sizing me up as if she thought I might do nicely as an hors-d'oeuvre.'

'Look,' said Faith, getting a grip on herself, and putting both hands on his chest to hold him at bay, 'this has gone quite far enough. Either you behave yourself, Max Kain, or you can pack your bags this minute. I offered you a place to stay because I'm grateful to you, and because you—well, because you deserve it after what you did at the Clambake. But if you can't keep your hands to yourself, the deal's off. I refuse to spend all my free time wondering when you're going to pounce next.'

'Wondering or hoping?' said Max, not moving.

'Don't flatter yourself. I'm not a pushover like Nellie, and I'm not at all anxious to attract your dubious attentions.'

'I see. And don't be uncharitable. Nellie enjoys the occasional compliment, that's all. I doubt if she gets many from her Ted.'

There was something in his eyes that puzzled her. It was almost as if he were seeing her in a way he hadn't expected and didn't like. It made her feel awkward, as if *she* were the one who had been toying with Nellie's affections. And what annoyed her particularly was the fact that he might just be right. Maybe a casual flirtation was exactly what the young nurse had needed to restore her confidence. Naturally Max *would* be the one to turn on his easy charm and do something about it.

'Oh, go away,' she said irritably. 'Take your hands off——'

'In case it's escaped your notice,' he interrupted, 'my hands aren't on you, Duchess. Yours, though, are very much on me.'

Faith glanced down. It was true. And she could feel his body heat through the T-shirt.

'All right,' she said, breathing deeply, 'you take your hands off the door and let me pass, and I'll take my hands off your chest. And from now on you'll keep your distance.'

'And what if I don't?' He still had that odd look in his eyes.

'If you don't, I'll——'

'Call Mrs Gruber?' he suggested. The words were light enough, but his voice was flat, almost distant.

'No,' she said. 'I'll call Constable Smith.'

To her surprised relief, Max gave a short, harsh laugh and moved away.

'Help yourself to the phone,' he said, gesturing.

'Oh, don't be ridiculous,' snapped Faith. Then, getting a grip on herself, 'Have you settled in?'

'What's to settle? I have about as much luggage as you have furniture.' He waved at a large khaki holdall in the corner. 'If it helps, I've hung up my jacket.'

And undone your trousers, thought Faith. From the corner of her eye she saw him fasten them, and heaved a quiet sigh of relief.

'What's for supper?' he asked, as he snapped his belt into place.

'I don't know. I suppose *you* didn't think to start anything?'

Max shook his head. 'I couldn't find the lupins.'

Faith put a hand over her mouth, choked, and managed to croak out gravely, 'I'm out of lupins. But there's a fresh pot of nasturtiums in the cupboard. Red ones.'

'Ah,' he nodded. 'I can hardly wait. Red ones, did you say?'

Their eyes met, and she saw that his were wary as well as amused.

'Yes,' she said, struck by an overwhelming need to get the better of him. 'You can help me prepare them. They'll go nicely with a soybean and avocado salad.'

She marched past him into the kitchen, and behind her she heard him swear softly.

'Is there some problem?' she asked over her shoulder, beginning to rummage in the fridge.

Max didn't answer, and when she straightened she saw he was leaning against the doorframe with a hand resting lightly above his head. The expression on his face was forbidding.

'No,' he said finally, 'no problem. No nasturtiums either.'

Faith shrugged. 'All right, we'll stick with the soybeans.'

'What we will actually do is eat out,' said Max, in the sort of voice that meant he didn't anticipate argument.

'The Clambake is closed until tomorrow. Because of the fire,' she smiled smugly.

'In that case we'll settle for Hal's Hamburgers.'

'I don't like Hal's Hamburgers.'

'Frankly, I don't give a damn what you like. I am not eating soybeans—or avocado.'

Neither was Faith. She didn't even have any in the apartment, but now that she'd started this farce, she wasn't about to let Max know that provoking him had been more on her mind than supper. 'That's too bad——' she began.

'It is, isn't it?'

She was just opening her mouth to tell him he could eat what he liked when he was by himself, but as long as he was staying with her he'd eat what *she* liked, when he took a step forward and curved both hands over her shoulders. Her mouth fell open, and she was still gaping up at him when he turned her round and began to propel her firmly in the direction of the door.

'Hey!' she exclaimed. 'What do you think you're doing?'

'Calling your bluff. You know perfectly well you weren't going to feed me beans for supper. On the other hand, I did offer you dinner the other night——'

'Max, I am not going out for dinner. I really don't like Hal's Hamburgers.'

'Neither do I. There's a quite civilised-looking restaurant down the highway. We'll go there.'

'But I'm still in my office clothes——'

'For which small mercy I'm deeply thankful. Don't even think of changing.'

'But——' she began.

'But nothing. For once, Faith Farraday, you're going to do exactly what you're told.' He reached round her waist and pulled the door open, shoving her out into the hall.

'My bag,' she protested.

'Here.' Without releasing her he bent down to pick up the bag which she'd conveniently left on the floor. She took it from him with an indignant scowl, and he shut the door behind him with a snap.

He kept his hands on her shoulders all the way down the stairs and across the parking area. When they reached the beige Ford he slid them down to her waist.

She tried to turn, but he unlocked the car and pressed her on to the seat. 'You're not going to try and run away on me now, are you?' he asked, looking down at her with his hand on the top of the door. He wore an affable but very determined smile.

Faith sighed. 'No,' she said. 'What's the point? You'd only kidnap me back. Besides, I'm hungry.'

'Good,' he said. 'Now stay put while I go and change.'

'But I haven't—you said...'

Max wasn't listening. In fact, he was already halfway across the tarmac. Faith had never known a man who moved so fast.

In less than ten minutes he was back, dressed in a dark, superbly pressed suit, a cream silk shirt and a red tie. Faith blinked. Impressive, expensive, dominant and *very* civilised. No longer the mountain man but a sexy, sophisticated powerhouse.

Involuntarily she licked her lips. 'Did all that come out of your bag?' she asked doubtfully.

'Most of it.'

She shook her head. 'I can't believe it. But I guess I'll have to.'

'That's what I like about you, Faith,' he said amiably. 'You know when to accept the inevitable—as in dinner with me. And, I hope, make the best of it.'

Faith thought of telling him she didn't see that there was likely to be any best about it, but she didn't, because it wouldn't be altogether true. The prospect of a safely public dinner with Max was a great deal less alarming than the idea of spending a whole evening alone with him. With luck, by the time they got home again it would be late enough for her to plead fatigue, and sequester herself in her bedroom.

As Max had said, the restaurant was new to the Peninsula. Faith hadn't been there before. It turned out to be fine dining of a style not previously found in the vicinity of Caley Cove—a converted Victorian mansion featuring crystal chandeliers, silver place settings and an atmosphere of old-style elegance and charm. On the walls were portraits of the founding family, bearded patriarchs and disapproving ladies who wouldn't have been caught dead on a beach with a banjo. Faith smiled to herself. The portraits might be intimidating, but somehow she wasn't intimidated. She felt relaxed for the first time that day.

There were only three other couples in the dining-room, and the service was discreet and efficient. When Max indicated by a subtle lift of his eyebrows that the two of them would like to be alone, the black-garbed waiter bowed and faded obligingly into the panelling.

'He probably thinks we're about to make love on the table,' Faith accused Max without stopping to think.

His teeth flashed white and wolfish. 'Does that worry you?'

It did, because the idea wasn't altogether unpleasant, but it hardly seemed wise to admit that. Not if she meant to keep him at arm's length.

'Not particularly,' she said coolly—and untruthfully. 'What does bother me is that you didn't give me time to change my clothes. I feel—underdressed.'

He ran his eyes appraisingly over her fitted navy suit and white blouse. 'Would that you were! Perhaps if we were to fulfil our waiter's expectations——'

'Expectations?'

'Of unconventional behaviour on the table.' He smiled wickedly.

Faith bit her lip in exasperation. 'Don't you ever think about anything but sex?'

'Who said I was thinking about sex?' Max broke off a piece of French bread and buttered it with irritating care.

The waiter passed by at that moment carrying wine to another table, so Faith didn't have to answer at once. By the time he was out of earshot she had had time to decide she wasn't going to. The conversation needed to be turned speedily in a more innocuous direction. The only trouble was, nothing about Max Kain seemed innocuous.

In the end, and greatly to her relief, Max was the one who turned the conversation. 'So you plan to stay in Caley Cove for two more years,' he murmured, in a changing-the-subject tone of voice.

'Who knows?' said Faith carelessly. 'I told you I usually take life as it comes.'

'No plans for the future?'

'You mean marriage and kids and all that, or some kind of high-powered career?'

'Either. Both.'

Faith shook her head. 'What will be will be. I did think of marrying once...' She stopped. She'd already told him about Stephen.

'And you will again.' Max frowned and picked up his wine glass. She wondered what she'd said to annoy him.

'What about you?' she asked, a little tartly. 'Are you going to spend the rest of your life climbing mountains?'

'For as long as I'm able. It's a way of life.' He was still frowning.

Faith was puzzled, and surprised by the brittle sound of her own voice when she asked with a quick toss of her head, 'No family ties for you, then, I imagine? A girl on every mountain, is that it?'

'Hardly. Most of my expeditions have enough complications as it is.'

'I see. So you take your pleasures where you find them. In between expeditions.' She knew she was goading him, but she couldn't stop herself.

'I'm not sure that my pleasures are any of your business. Yet.' The word was weighted with meaning.

'But since you ask, yes, there have been one or two very temporary ladies in my life.'

'Who faded conveniently out of your life when you were through with them,' she gibed.

'No, I faded conveniently out of theirs when I was through with them.'

Yes, Faith could imagine. Max, the footloose mountaineer, would never permit the love of a woman to tie him down. Hearth and home, children, would be shackles to a man like him. And any woman dumb enough to fall for him would deserve all the grief she was bound to get.

Faith wondered why the gourmet delight of her plate tasted unexpectedly bitter.

Max was unusually silent throughout the rest of the meal, and she felt disinclined to talk much herself. The tension that had been between them from the moment they met on the beach was almost tangible now, and it was an angry tension, as though one wrong word from either of them could easily ignite an explosion.

'Right,' said Max harshly, the moment she had drained the last of her tea, 'time to go home.'

Out of sheer contrariness, Faith wanted to demand another pot of tea, and she had to force herself to remember that she was a mature, sensible adult, not a little girl who threw tantrums. Besides, as she glanced at the hard line of Max's jaw, it occurred to her that in his present mood he wasn't likely to put up with any tantrum.

The tension was still between them, if possible even more pronounced, when Faith unlocked the door to her apartment. Max followed her in without speaking, and when she made straight for the refuge of her bedroom he disappeared into the bathroom. She could hear him running water and splashing as she pulled on her red cotton nightgown and covered it with a blue and red robe.

When she finally emerged, Max was standing in the middle of the room wearing only his dark trousers.

'Where do I sleep?' he asked abruptly, beginning to unbuckle his belt.

'Er...' Faith swallowed hard. 'Anywhere you like.' When he glanced pointedly at her bedroom door she added quickly, 'I mean here, in the living-room. Help yourself to the cushions.'

Their eyes met. 'Have you—er—got everything you want?' Faith asked inanely.

'No,' answered Max, 'but I've got everything I expected to get. Why? Are you about to make me an offer I can't refuse?'

She'd sure left herself open for that one. 'I don't know,' she said, pretending not to understand him. 'I see you found the blankets, but I wondered if you wanted anything else before I go. Towels, a toothbrush, something to drink...' She pulled nervously at the sash of her robe.

'No, thank you.' Max looked at his watch. 'Do you always go to bed this early?'

'Sometimes. When I'm tired.'

'And at the moment you're tired of my company.' He fixed her with a look so chilling she had to bite back a gasp.

'Yes,' she admitted, rallying, and returning the look with interest, 'very tired. I'm sorry, but——'

'No need to be sorry. You've provided me with a bed for the night.'

She blinked, surprised by this sudden docility, which didn't sound at all like the authoritative man she was becoming used to. Did it mean she was actually going to escape without any further protest from him? It seemed almost too good to be true.

It was.

As she turned away mumbling a muffled goodnight, she felt a firm hand on her arm. She jerked round as if she'd been jolted by lightning. As, in one way, she had.

'What's the matter, Faith?' demanded Max. 'Don't you trust me?'

'No!' Faith made an effort to lower her voice. 'No, I don't. Can you give me one reason why I should?'

'I think so.'

To her consternation, instead of launching into a confident catalogue of his own virtues, Max put both arms around her waist and pulled her to him.

She started to struggle, but at once he bent his head, pressed his lips over hers and began to rotate the tips of his fingers in slow, erotic circles just below the base of her spine. The lightning she had sensed earlier forked and sizzled through her body, making her cry out with a desire for him that knocked all her inhibitions to the ground. In the space of a few seconds she had become clay, soft and mindless in his arms, as if she could only be brought to life by his touch.

She returned his kiss with a frantic abandon that reflected her instinctive knowledge that with Max the needs of the moment were all she could ever hope to fulfil. There could be no future. Only now.

He enfolded her more tightly in his embrace, moved his lips over her face and down her neck until he encountered the prim ruffled collar of her nightgown. And then, incredibly, as her fingers kneaded the muscles of his naked back, he lifted his head, rested his hands lightly on her hips and held her away.

'Is that reason enough?' he asked softly.

'Reason?' She gazed at him blankly, her heart jumping as if it struggled to escape from her chest. Her lungs were almost empty of breath.

'Mmm.' He sounded a little breathless himself. 'Reason to trust me.'

'I—I don't understand.' Faith ran a hand across her forehead and discovered her hair was plastered to it damply.

'Don't you? I thought you were convinced I intended to—how did you put it?—take my pleasures where I found them? And I could have, couldn't I? But I didn't.'

'Oh, God.' Faith stared at him, no longer mindless with desire, but numb with disbelief at her own behaviour. He was right, of course. He could have taken her here, on the cushions, in her bedroom or anywhere else he chose. And she wouldn't have protested. She would have welcomed his lovemaking, encouraged him. Loved him back. Only—only it wasn't love, was it? It was plain, unembellished physical need, and no euphemistic phrases could alter that.

Faith lifted her head. The truth, because it was the truth, must be faced. 'Yes,' she said, 'you could have done anything you wanted. Why didn't you?'

Max stared at her for a moment and then turned his head away. 'Damned if I know.' His voice was hard, with an edge to it that sounded like frustration. 'I suppose I wanted to prove that you could trust me.'

'Maybe,' said Faith, clasping her hands behind her back, 'maybe you didn't really want to.'

He gave a harsh bark of laughter. 'Angling for compliments, Duchess? You know I want to.'

Yes, in a way, she knew that. But he *hadn't* taken advantage, and it didn't really make any sense. In fact, both of them wanted the same thing, and there was no reason why they shouldn't have it. Yet they were fighting it every inch of the way. At least she was. She still wasn't sure about him.

Quite suddenly she felt she couldn't bear to be in the same room with him a second longer. He was still turned away from her, his fists bunched at his thighs, and she was afraid that, if she didn't get away, instead of fleeing she would fling her arms around him, pull him to her and try to smooth the angry furrows from his brow.

'Goodnight, Max,' she said quickly, and scurried for the safety of her room.

Once again he caught up with her, spun her around and kissed her. But this time his kiss just touched her cheek, and it had all the passion of a brother kissing his sister goodnight. Then he opened the bedroom door, pushed her in quite gently, and shut it behind her.

Blindly Faith stumbled over to her bed. When her knees came up against the edge she fell on to the covers and buried her face in the consoling warmth of the pillow.

What was happening to her? Why did she feel as if she'd just been kicked in the teeth? As she had told Max on more than one occasion, she had always been the kind of person who took life's punches on the chin and then bounced back. As she had been forced to do after Stephen.

As she would after Max?

Only with Max there would be nothing to bounce back from. He had kissed her twice, she had responded, and it looked as though that was as far as it would go.

She lifted her head, twisted the corner of the sheet into a knot, and rolled over. This was nonsense. Either she had an affair with Max, which would, of necessity, be brief, or she didn't. She knew the decision rested with her. She also knew that an affair was all she could hope for.

That thought made her sit up. Did she want more? Was that what was eating away at her, destroying her peace of mind? Faith groaned out loud. Oh, no, not again. Please, not again. She *couldn't* have fallen in love with Maxwell Kain. Surely she wasn't that stupid?

You've made worse mistakes, a small voice murmured in her head. Remember Stephen?

Oh, yes, she remembered Stephen. And compared to Stephen, Max was a knight on a white charger. Max admitted to being a bit of an opportunist, to being single-minded in pursuit of his own ends. He was impatient too. But he was strong as well as honest, he hadn't even thought of his own safety when he'd rescued Nate Spellman and his wife, he'd been a wonderful influence on Bruce and...

Oh, dear lord, what was the sense in trying to fool herself? Of all people? Faith ran a hand through her hair.

In spite of her sensible resolutions, she had fallen in love with Max Kain. There was no doubt about it. Hook, line and sinker, and, almost from the moment they'd met, she had known that Max was destined to change her life.

She had never loved Stephen that way.

Which meant that if she let Max make love to her, life would be a thousand times more unbearable when he left.

She closed her eyes and fell back on to the pillows. She was so lost in thought, so shattered and disbelieving, that she didn't hear the sound of a man's fist thudding against the other side of the wall.

And if she had, she wouldn't have cared.

'Damn,' said Max softly, shifting his shoulders on the cushions. 'Damn, damn, damn. What in hell have you gone and done now, Kain, you bloody fool?'

He turned on his back and stared balefully up at the white ceiling. He knew what he'd done all right. He'd broken the rule of a lifetime and allowed a pair of innocent violet eyes to touch his heart. And if he wasn't careful those eyes could bind him with silken threads so strong that cutting them might very well be devastating. For himself that wasn't important; he was used to enduring pain and risk. But he had no desire to hurt the essentially gentle and generous young woman who had invited him into her home.

Only he knew that in the end he *would* cut those threads. Ruthlessly. He would have no choice.

He swore under his breath and pushed a hand through his hair. There was only one thing to do—restore the rules. Operate the way he always had. Yes, tomorrow he would see that matters were put back on their usual footing. It wouldn't be any problem. The Duchess in there had left him in no doubt that she didn't think much of him or his lifestyle, but that she could easily be persuaded into his bed. As long as he took care that she understood, didn't expect more than he could give... Faith was kind and carefree, honest and—yes, often ag-

gravating. But she would see things his way. He'd make
sure of it.

Max glanced at his watch in the moonlight coming
through the window. Well after midnight. She'd be asleep
now. Yes, better leave it till tomorrow.

Faith stared through the glass at a wild canary singing
on her sill and wished she didn't feel so exhausted. She
hadn't slept well, but her alarm had gone fifteen minutes
ago, and she really had no choice but to get up.

With luck, Max would still be asleep, and if she was
very quiet perhaps she might just manage to slip out of
the apartment without waking him.

She had toast and orange juice but went without her
morning tea because the whistle of the kettle was very
loud. She was equally cautious when she pulled open the
bedroom door after changing into her businesslike black
suit.

Max was lying on a pile of cushions with his chest
bare to the waist, and to Faith's relief he appeared to
be deeply asleep. She held her breath and tiptoed past
him with her shoes clutched in one hand.

Made it, she thought, as her feet came level with his
knees.

But she had counted her chickens too soon. Just as
she lifted her right foot to take another cautious step
forward, a large hand closed around her ankle.

'Well, well, well,' drawled a sleepy male voice from
the floor. 'I was dreaming that it was a bright, sunny
day and I was sitting on a riverbank fishing. What a
very nice catch to wake up to.'

CHAPTER SIX

FAITH, because she had no choice, came to an undignified halt.

'Let go of me,' she demanded. 'Max, I have to get to work, and I'm in a hurry.'

Max smiled lazily. 'Mmm, but I'm not. Tell your boss you need a day off.'

'A day off for what?'

'Good behaviour?'

'Don't be ridiculous.'

'OK, how about you need time off to entertain a guest who'd otherwise be bored, bereft and lonely?' He rubbed his thumb gently down her calf.

'I offered you a place to sleep,' said Faith, wishing his touch didn't feel so right, 'not a song-and-dance routine.'

'I wasn't thinking of singing and dancing. I had something more stimulating in mind.'

'I'll bet,' snapped Faith. 'Max, let go this minute or I'll be late. Besides, you said you have work to do as well.'

He sighed. 'All right, if you insist, I suppose I can wait until this evening to be entertained.' He released her ankle with overplayed reluctance and cast a reproachful look up at her scowling face.

She glared at him and stepped quickly out of harm's way. 'I told you I wasn't in the entertainment business,' she said sharply.

When his only answer was a devastatingly attractive leer, some instinct made her reverse direction and hurry back to her bedroom. When she reappeared she was carrying her banjo.

Max raised his eyebrows. 'Music while you work?' he enquired.

Instead of replying, Faith took a circuitous route to the door and hurried out into the hall and down the stairs.

'What's eating you?' asked Angela, looking up from her desk the moment her secretary stamped into the office. 'Max Kain again?'

'You might say so,' said Faith, standing her banjo in the corner and throwing her bag down beside it. 'He's impossible, Angela. He even told me to take the day off because he's bored.'

'You should have,' said Angela. 'I could have got Sarah Malone—Jackson, I mean—to come in. Her mother would have taken little Caroline.'

'You're no help,' grumbled Faith. 'I don't know why I ever told him he could stay.'

Angela glanced at her shrewdly. 'He's a very attractive man, isn't he? Famous too. There was a whole programme about him on TV when he climbed Mount Everest.'

'Was there? I'd never heard of him before.' Faith was defensive.

'Well, you have now. And I suspect you'd like to hang on to him. You could do worse.'

'Not a chance. Though there was a moment last night...' Faith's voice trailed off, and when she spoke again it was on a lighter, less wistful note. 'Anyway, he's the Roving Romeo again this morning, all predatory and waiting and male. Ready to seize the first opportunity that comes along.'

'An opportunity like Faith Farraday, for instance?'

'It looks that way.' Faith stalked into her office and thumped herself down behind her desk. She stared down at the Rosenthal contract without seeing one word that was printed.

Was she being a fool? Max would leave her, of course, and quite soon. But that was no reason to deny herself happiness now. A week or two of loving Max might be better than not loving him at all.

So why was she hesitating? It wasn't like her. She hadn't hesitated once she realised she loved Stephen. She picked up a pen and stabbed it into her blotter. Only— perhaps she *hadn't* really loved Stephen. What she felt for Max was so very different...

And when Max left her, the world would be an emptier place.

She was still hesitating when she finished work that evening, and when it came time to go home she knew she didn't want to. She also knew what instinct had prompted her to grab her banjo that morning. It was the instinct of self-preservation.

Bidding Angela a hasty goodnight, she hurried down the cliff road to the sea.

'What in hell do you think you're doing?' Max's voice behind her was almost conversational, but Faith didn't need any psychology degree to know he wasn't amused.

'What does it look like?' she asked, playing a final soft chord on her banjo. After it was carried away on the breeze she let her fingers rest lightly on the strings.

'Evasion. Running away.'

'Running away? From what?' She stared at the waves rippling like sheets of molten gold in the evening sun.

'Me, I suppose.'

'Why should I run away from you?'

'That's what I came to find out.'

Faith turned around then and stared up into his face. No, Max was definitely not amused. His jaw was thrust out, his grey eyes hard, and she had a feeling he'd like to pick her up and shake her.

'For your information,' she told him coldly, 'I'm just doing what I often do in the evenings. I fail to see why I should change my habits for you.'

His lips tightened, but for a moment she thought she saw a shadow fall across his face. Then he hooked his thumbs in his belt and said derisively, 'The perfect hostess, aren't you, Duchess? Why did you invite me to stay?'

Faith bit her lip. 'Because you were kind to Bruce. And because Caley Cove owes you something.'

'So I've been told by the Mayor, Constable Smith, half a dozen volunteer firemen—and a lady called Clara Malone. All of whom offered me a place to stay. As far as I'm concerned, nobody owes me a thing.'

Faith gasped. 'Are you saying that all those people would have taken you in and fed you? And yet you had the nerve to let me think you'd have to find some other quiet place to work if I didn't help out?' She put down her banjo and jumped up. 'Maxwell Kain, you are the most deceitful, conniving, manipulative...' She stopped, searching for a more pointed word to express her feelings.

'Perfidious? Treacherous? Underhanded?' he suggested helpfully.

'Yes, all of them,' she snapped.

'Why? Because I chose the best offer?'

'Because . . .' She stopped. Why *was* she so angry with Max?

'At a loss for words?' he asked interestedly.

Faith stared at him, heard the sea tumbling on to the sand behind her and felt as if she'd been deflated like a plastic beach ball. 'Yes, I guess I am,' she said tiredly. 'Come on, let's go home.'

She picked up her banjo, and the shoes which sat beside it on her log, and began to make her way up to the road.

Max strode beside her, and when she glanced up at him she saw that he looked more thoughtful now than angry.

She supposed she couldn't blame him, because she *had* been behaving like an idiot. There had been absolutely no point in coming to the beach just so she could avoid a guest who would be waiting for her as soon as she got home—whether it was five-thirty or midnight. Waiting for his supper too, no doubt, she thought resignedly. Probably hunger had driven him to pursue her to the beach.

But when she unlocked the door to her apartment, her nose was immediately assaulted by the smell of food. At least, she supposed it was food.

'What have you been doing?' she asked with deep suspicion. 'Brewing spells?'

'Mmm. Eye of newt and toe of frog. But I'm afraid it's cold now.'

'Oh,' said Faith faintly. Was *that* why Max had been so annoyed with her for not coming home? 'Er—did you say eye of newt?'

'I did. Along with wool of bat and tongue of dog. I hope that appeals to you.'

'Almost as much as adder's fork and blindworm's sting, lizard's leg and howlet's wing,' said Faith drily. 'Are you partial to Shakespearean cooking?'

Max took her arm and led her into the kitchen. 'It has its appeal,' he admitted. 'Especially the lizard's leg.'

Faith shuddered, and he brushed a hand over his mouth.

A large stewpot sat on the stove looking as if it had recently been turned off. She lifted the lid gingerly.

The pot contained a greenish-brown mixture that resembled algae except that its colour was darker. As Faith stared at it with foreboding, she noticed a transparent lump in the middle that could very well pass for eye of newt.

'What is it?' she asked, trying not to show her revulsion.

'Bodger's Special Vegetarian Trail Food,' said Max complacently. 'I found an outdoor shop in Port Angeles, so I stocked up.' When Faith said nothing, he turned up the heat and continued, 'I thought you might enjoy the change from lupins. Besides, it's the only thing I know how to cook.'

'Vegetarian Trail Food?' gulped Faith. 'That's what you live on?'

'Oh, no. I can manage Bodger's Curried Meat, Bodger's Goulash, Bodger's Chilli Con Carne for Hikers...'

Faith got the picture.

'Do we—er—eat anything with it?' she asked nervously.

'Sure—bread. I bought a loaf from the bakery.'

She heaved a sigh of relief. Starvation wasn't inevitable after all.

When Max set a bowl of his green mixture in front of her she almost beat an ignominious retreat. But she saw him looking at her as if he expected her to do just that. Recollecting that she was made of sterner stuff, she forced herself to swallow a mouthful.

'Hmm, it's not bad,' she admitted grudgingly.

It wasn't good either, but she wasn't about to give Max the satisfaction of watching her choke. She studied him more closely and saw that in spite of her efforts, he knew very well what she was thinking—and was thoroughly enjoying her discomfiture.

'I am,' she said through her teeth, 'resisting an urge to dump this bowl of glop on your head only with enormous difficulty, Max Kain.'

'Go ahead,' he replied, swallowing a mouthful of glop. 'Of course, if you do, I'll have to take my clothes off. They'll need washing.'

Faith lowered her gaze and did her best to quell a sudden shiver of excitement. 'In that case I'll let you off,' she said quickly.

'I was afraid you would.' Max finished his meal with evident enjoyment and waited for her to finish hers.

'Would you like coffee?' she asked, when she could find no further excuse to concentrate her attention on food. 'I've got some now.'

'No, thank you,' said Max, leaning back and folding his arms. 'I'd like you.'

'Me?' Her voice was a high-pitched squeak.

'Mmm. I didn't mind waiting until you'd eaten, but now it's time for some serious entertainment. It's been a very dull day without you, Duchess.'

'Well, that's just too bad.' Faith couldn't believe what she was hearing, and she pushed her chair back from the table and stood up. 'What's the matter with you, Max? Why have you gone all predatory on me again? I thought you said I could trust you.'

'You can,' he said, standing too. 'But can you trust yourself? As to *why*—because I want you, of course. And as you've shown me you want me just as much, can you think of a reason in the world why we shouldn't entertain each other? Provided, of course, that both of us can accept the inevitable limitations.'

'Limitations?'

He nodded, his eyes very steady on hers. 'Yes. I'm leaving soon. You know I won't be back, don't you?'

Yes, she knew that. And if she agreed to his proposition, what did that make her? Just another of Max Kain's passing fancies. For a little while she *had* hoped he felt more, but the look on his face now was almost uninterested, as if her answer didn't matter to him much. And he sounded so brisk, so businesslike, as though seduction was a standard routine. As perhaps, for him, it was. And yet last night...

Faith fumbled with a button on her jacket. Last night Max had been different. He had seemed more human, as if he had doubts about himself like everyone else. And he had kissed her as a brother might kiss his sister.

'Why have you changed your mind?' she asked finally.

'Changed my mind? I haven't.'

'Yes, you have. You were right when you said you could have taken me last night. But you didn't.'

He raised an eyebrow. 'And you think I might now? Are you suggesting that I'm about to ravish you on the kitchen counter, amid the remains of Bodger's Special Stew?'

She shook her head dumbly.

'Quite right, I'm not. The decision is yours.' He held out his arms. 'Come here, Duchess.'

Faith, her gaze fixed on the expanse of soft grey wool across his chest, took an automatic step backwards.

'Wrong way,' said Max laconically. 'I'm over here.'

'I can see that.' Her throat felt dry, her pulses were pounding and she couldn't tear her gaze from his eyes.

He smiled then, a confident, full-lipped, utterly magnetic smile that caused her to lose all sense of caution, all sense of any reality except the sinuous forearms of the man standing in front of her. They were a magician's arms, irresistible, reaching for her, issuing a command she couldn't refuse.

The decision she had been wrestling with all day wasn't an issue any more. As she had unconsciously known all along, what was about to happen had been inevitable right from the beginning.

Slowly, her eyes locked with his, she moved round the table, and when she came up to him he took her into his arms.

They stayed like that for several seconds, not moving, just breathing in the scent of each other's bodies. Then Max loosened his grip, ran his hands deliciously down her sides and over her hips and thighs, smoothing the tight fabric of her skirt. A shudder ran through her, and she moaned, pushing her hands up under his grey sweater to feel the hard muscles of his chest and the beating of his heart beneath her fingers.

'You're beautiful, Duchess,' he whispered, beginning to undo the buttons of her prim black jacket.

'So are you,' she murmured. 'Oh, Max, please...'

'Please what?' he asked huskily, sliding the jacket off her shoulders and tossing it on to the floor.

Faith raised her eyes, saw dishes stacked on the counter and a smear of green algae on the cupboard.

'Please kiss me,' she said. 'But not here.'

He caught her wrists, pulled them against his thighs and stared down at her. 'Faith,' he said softly, 'do you mean——?'

'Oh, yes,' breathed Faith. 'Yes, yes, yes. Please...'

With a muffled laugh, because his mouth was pressed against her hair, Max scooped her up in his arms and bore her out into the living room.

'I—I've only a single bed,' she murmured.

'Not an insuperable barrier,' he assured her, moving his lips to her ear. 'Why do you have all these cushions, if not for...?' He paused, and there was no need for him to finish the sentence.

'For love?' she said. 'Of course.' And then, breathlessly, as he laid her down on a bed of multi-coloured checks, 'Why didn't I think of that?'

He smiled and propped himself on one elbow beside her. 'Because you were too busy playing the Duchess.' There was just a hint of censure in his tone. 'And that's one role I don't want to see you in again.'

Faith took his face in her hands and laughed up at him. 'Why not? She's the only one who could ever keep you in order.'

'Cheeky witch!' He put his hand on her breast and began to stroke it through the thin silk blouse.

She gasped and turned towards him, and in a moment the blouse was on the floor. So was her skirt. She put a hand on his waist, began to unfasten his belt. And then there was nothing between them, she was in his arms, and he was kissing her with a wildness that excited her, challenged her and reminded her fleetingly that this was a man of the mountains who lived roughly, perhaps loved roughly...

But in the end he took her with an exquisitely gentle expertise that left her crying out to him to claim her. Now, before she was driven mad with longing.

And he did, and when it was over Faith felt as if she were the one who had climbed a mountain. The most rugged, beautiful, exhilarating mountain in the world, from whose summit she could see vistas of such un-dreamed-of loveliness that tears brimmed up in her eyes and fell in gentle rivulets down her cheeks.

'You're crying.' Max ran a finger along her cheekbone. 'What is it, Faith? Wasn't it——?'

'It was wonderful.' She sniffed loudly and buried her face against his shoulder.

He put a hand under her chin and made her look at him. 'Then why are you crying?'

'Because—because I'm happy.' She gave another loud sniff and stared at the face so close to hers with a mixture of love and defiance.

Seeing that look, Max frowned. 'Do you always cry when you're happy?'

Faith wondered why the voice which a moment before had been so tender now sounded clipped and abrupt. 'No,' she said simply. 'This is the first time.'

For some reason she didn't understand, her answer only made the furrows between his eyebrows deepen. 'Faith,' he said, drawing away from her to stare with empty eyes across the room, 'I thought you understood.'

'Understood?' She ran a finger over the hard angles of his cheekbone.

'That I have to leave town in a week. Or two at the most. That I won't be back.'

She pulled her hand against her face as if he'd slapped her. 'Yes,' she said, after a long, tense silence, 'of course I understand that.'

He nodded and rolled over on to his back. 'Just so long as you do,' he said, folding an arm behind his head.

Faith lay beside him, not touching him, staring up at the ceiling. What was Max trying to tell her? That she was just a handy female body, someone to satisfy his hungers until it came time for him to leave? Well, in a way, she'd known that all along, hadn't she? Although she had thought he liked her as well. But she hadn't gone into this with her eyes closed, and it wasn't *that* which made her want to hit him, to wound him as he had wounded her. It was his callous lack of thought for her feelings. He'd seen her crying, foreseen future problems for himself, and promptly destroyed a perfect moment just so that he wouldn't be inconvenienced by a woman who might feel she had a right to expect more from him than a quick roll on the cushions—more than the casual satisfaction of a physical need.

His fingers touched her hair, tugged it gently, until she was forced to look at him again. 'Faith,' he said, 'I never promised you——'

'A rose garden? No, you certainly didn't.' Faith sat up, brushing the back of her hand across her eyes. 'Whatever made you think I wanted your promises, Max? I'm well aware how easily those can be broken.'

'Yes, I suppose you are. I should have remembered.' He smiled, a crooked, sardonic sort of smile that, strangely, tugged at her heart. 'In that case, it seems neither of us has much to lose.'

He sounded so bleak and bitter that, without really meaning to, Faith found herself touching his face, running a finger over his lips to make his mouth gentle again.

Max groaned and reached up to curve his hand round the back of her neck. Again without meaning to respond, she bent over him, and began to trail mothlike kisses across the hard line of his jaw. And she knew, without any doubt, that, whatever Max might say, she had everything to lose if she allowed him to become part of her life. Even if it was only for a week or two. And there had been something in his eyes a moment ago that frightened her a little. A sort of cynicism, a hard enigmatic glaze that made her think he was determined not to let her come too close. He didn't want the love she had to give.

She started to pull away from him, wanting, and yet not wanting, to escape. But just as on those other occasions, she couldn't do it. Her need for Max was too great.

He was responding to her kisses now, moving his hands up and down her spine. She cried out softly.

And then he was loving her again, with a passionate, all-consuming hunger that set her blood and every part of her on fire.

When at last they came together, Faith knew that the world and her life had changed forever. But this time the view from the mountain was one of ice and sharp peaks.

'Faith?' murmured Max a few minutes later, as she lay with her eyes closed not looking at him. 'Faith...?'

'That's me,' she whispered, still lost on the mountain, but aware that reality beckoned. 'What—what can I do for you?'

'You've already done it,' he said, tracing his thumb across her forehead. 'Most satisfactorily too.'

He spoke neutrally, but Faith felt a sudden sharp pain and came back to earth with a bump. So she'd performed satisfactorily, had she? Provided him with the entertainment he needed . . . ?

She lay still a few moments longer, then without leaving herself time to think, she pushed his hand away and stumbled awkwardly on to her feet. When Max reached for her she grabbed her clothes and hurried into the bedroom.

'Faith!' The roar that followed her wasn't neutral at all, it was angry.

She ignored him.

Sitting on the edge of her bed wrapped in a blanket, she listened to him try the handle of her door. She had locked it. Then she listened to the colourful stream of language that followed. Max's travels certainly hadn't left him short in the vocabulary department. After that, she waited until she heard him move away. When part of him, his fist presumably, slammed against something hard, she heard Mrs Gruber's broom-handle hit the ceiling with malicious vigour.

Faith listened for a while and then, hearing nothing further, she grabbed a long yellow hostess gown from the cupboard, tiptoed to the door, and pulled it open.

Max was seated against the wall wearing only his trousers. His arms were crossed, and he was glaring stony-eyed at a blank TV screen. He glanced up when she came out, but made no effort to halt her passage to the bathroom.

Faith took a long, cool shower, and when she emerged into the living-room at last, decently garbed in the yellow gown, her head was held high and her eyes were as cold as mauve glass.

'Oh, God,' muttered Max, who was still glaring grimly into space, 'the Duchess again? What in hell have I done this time?'

His eyes weren't any warmer than hers.

Faith stared at him. Didn't he *know* what he'd done? Was he so self-centred he didn't even realise that the moment to remind a woman he was leaving her was not when they had just made love, most beautifully, and she was lying warm and happy in his arms? Well, if he didn't, he was about to find out. She had never been one to play games, and, if something needed saying, she said it.

'What you've done,' she told him, holding her hands rigidly at her sides, 'is make me feel used. As if I'm just a satisfactory body you decided to grab on to in passing.'

His mouth, which had been trap-like in the first place, tightened further. 'I didn't have to grab it,' he said flatly. 'It was offered—enthusiastically.'

'Yes, and accepted, used, and lightly tossed away.'

His eyes narrowed, and she could tell he was startled as well as angry.

'Tossed away? What are you talking about, Faith? I thought we both wanted the same thing. Why would I toss you away?'

'Oh, not now. Not immediately,' she said scornfully. 'But you took great care to make sure I understood you weren't for keeps.'

Max shook his head, and settled his shoulders more firmly against the wall. He reminded her of a lion who thought his prey was assured, and then discovered it has somehow eluded him.

'You always knew I wasn't for keeps,' he said wearily.

'Yes, but I didn't need you to rub my nose in it. Not then.'

He frowned, unfolded his body slowly, and stood up. 'Faith, what is this? I thought you understood. And when I first met you, you assured me most emphatically that you weren't in the market for a replacement for Stephen——'

'I'm not,' said Faith quickly.

'Then why do I get the impression...?' He ran a hand through his hair and made what looked like a conscious effort to wipe all emotion from his face. 'OK, so my impression was wrong. You're no more interested in long-term plans than I am. Have I got that right?'

'Quite right.'

'Good. But reminding you that our time together will, of necessity, be brief, was tactless of me? Is that it?'

Yes, that was partly it, but not all. The problem, quite simply, was that she loved him, and couldn't bear the thought of his leaving. But she couldn't tell him that. Not now when he'd made it plain he wouldn't stay. Her pride wouldn't let her tell the truth.

'I suppose so,' she said offhandedly, starting to move towards the kitchen.

He caught her arm. 'Faith, don't be an idiot. If I've offended you, or my timing was bad, I'm sorry—truly. It was just that for a moment there I thought...'

'You thought I intended to play the clinging vine.'

He took a deep breath, and she could see he was trying to control his frustration. 'I don't know what I thought. Except that I wanted to be sure you understood. Don't have the vapours on me, Duchess.'

'I'm not,' she said crisply, fighting down the urge to scratch his face. 'And as apologies go, I've heard better. Never mind; for the sake of peace in the home, I'll accept it.'

The look he gave her made her frown. It was exasperated, but at the same time confused. And deep in the grey eyes she thought she read a question, an uncertainty she hadn't seen there before. Was it a kind of pain? Or guilt? No, Max wasn't the kind of man who showed pain. Sometimes she suspected he only acknowledged it when battling the elements on his mountains. And he was too confident, too assured, too set on his own path to have time for guilt.

Judging by his next words, she was right.

'OK,' he said abruptly, 'crisis over. If that's what it was.'

'It wasn't.' Faith shook his hand off her arm and made her way into the kitchen. 'Do you want coffee?'

'That's all I'm going to get, isn't it?'

'Yes, I'm afraid it is,' she said, wishing she didn't feel like crying.

'All right, then I'll settle for coffee. Though I'm still not entirely sure what I've done to turn you back into Caley Cove's resident Duchess.'

'You haven't done anything,' snapped Faith. 'I think I made a mistake, that's all.'

'Ah, so now I'm a mistake, am I?'

The unpleasant edge to his voice made her wince, and she dropped a coffee-mug on to the floor with a crash.

It shattered into a hundred orange shards, and Mrs Gruber pounded loudly beneath them.

'Yes,' she said through her teeth, 'a grave mistake.'

Max watched as she picked up the pieces. She could feel his gaze burning into her neck. But he didn't offer to help her, and when she finally stood up he was lounging in the doorway, looking as though he was enjoying the entertainment.

Irritably Faith threw the debris into the waste-bin and finished making the coffee. She handed him a mug without speaking and carried her own cup of tea out to the living-room. After setting it carefully on the floor, she made straight for the TV and switched it on.

Max waited until she had settled her back against the wall and, without waiting for an invitation, lowered himself down beside her.

'I gather we're to spend a cosy evening on the floor watching television,' he gibed. 'What do you have planned for tomorrow?'

Oh, yes, tomorrow. She'd forgotten the weekend was upon them.

'Will you still be here tomorrow?' she asked, in as careless a tone as she could manage.

'Would you rather I wasn't?'

No, she wouldn't rather he wasn't. But if the atmosphere between them was going to remain as it was now, all tense and edged with sparks and accusations, it might be better if he left—however much it tore at her heart to see him go.

'Yes, perhaps you...' She couldn't say it. 'It's up to you,' she managed finally, trying desperately to sound indifferent.

'Is it?' He leaned his head back, and when she looked at him she saw that his eyes were closed and that there was a rigidity about his mouth that she hadn't noticed before. But after a while he turned his steady grey gaze on her and said with a complete lack of emphasis, 'All right, in that case I'll stay.' Faith released her breath and then drew it in again quickly when he added, 'Do you suppose that particular contortion can be duplicated?'

She realised he was looking at the very explicit love scene that was taking place on the screen. So she changed the channel.

They spent the rest of the evening sitting side by side on the cushions gazing with apparent absorption at a documentary on pigs. Faith had always had a fondness for the placid, flat-nosed creatures, but she had a feeling that Max's attention was elsewhere. Although he didn't mention tomorrow again, or make any reference to what had happened between them, once or twice she caught him glancing sideways at her with a kind of controlled frustration. She found his glances ridiculously disconcerting—especially in view of the fact that only a short time ago she had lain blissfully entwined in his arms.

At eleven o'clock she remarked with unconvincing carelessness that she supposed it was time to go to bed.

'Alone?' enquired Max, as if her answer mattered to him, but not excessively.

Faith, who had been asking herself the same question for most of the evening, found she had no ready answer.

She didn't want to go to bed alone, she wanted to lie here on the cushions with Max. But she was afraid. Usually, if no one would be hurt by her actions, she tended to do as she wanted. But in this case she was convinced someone would be hurt, and as that person was herself, she hesitated.

'I think it *would* be better,' she said carefully, after an overlong pause. 'Don't you?'

She stopped breathing, hoping and yet fearing he would argue. Instead he picked up her hand, stared at it for a moment, then gazed intently into her eyes. She didn't know what he expected to see there, but she fought to maintain a non-committal expression.

After what seemed an aeon he dropped her fingers again and replied in a heartbreakingly detached voice, 'Yes, perhaps it would.'

She nodded and staggered awkwardly to her feet. Then, turning her back, she left him with a whispered, 'Goodnight.'

'Goodnight, Duchess.' Max's dispassionate murmur followed her into the bedroom.

And why shouldn't he be dispassionate? she thought bitterly. His bodily needs have been satisfied for the moment. So have mine, for that matter. But as for my emotional needs—well, I guess they never will be. She closed her eyes and groaned softly. Dear God, how in the world was she going to get through the next two weeks?

She pulled off the yellow gown, slipped into a night-dress, and lay down on her narrow bed, expecting to lie awake for hours.

But she didn't. The moment her head hit the pillow, her eyes closed, and when she opened them again the rays of the morning sun were streaming through the window and the smell of coffee was seeping under her door.

She rubbed her eyelids, grabbed her robe, and without troubling to look in the mirror, stumbled out into the kitchen.

An empty package of Bodger's Quick Pancake Mix lay on the table, and, judging from the brisk motions of Max's wrists and the encouraging sizzling sounds coming from the stove, breakfast was well under way.

He turned round when he heard her come in, and she saw him take a deep breath. 'What a waste,' he murmured, waving the egg-turner at her.

'Waste? What do you mean?'

'You look all warm and soft and sleepy. Ready for bed, not breakfast.'

'I just got out of bed.'

'I know. More's the pity.'

'Stop it, Max,' snapped Faith, wanting to say something else entirely.

'Yes,' he said bleakly, turning back to the stove, 'you're right. It's impossible, isn't it?'

'What is?'

'You. Me. This situation.' He flipped two pancakes expertly on to a plate and gestured at her to sit down.

Too dazed to argue, she sat. 'Yes,' she agreed, staring at the neat round pancakes he placed in front of her, 'I guess it is.'

He put down another plate and sat across from her, resting his arms on the table. 'Right,' he said, with a briskness that appalled her, 'so we have to come to a decision, don't we? I can stay here and share your bed— or perhaps I should say cushions. I can stay here, not share your bed, and be driven crazy by a woman who behaves like a Duchess and looks like an invitation to paradise remembered. Or I can leave at once. I don't propose to exercise the second option, so which is it to be, Duchess? And eat your pancakes, please, before they get cold.'

CHAPTER SEVEN

FAITH picked up her fork automatically. Put the way Max had just put it, what possible decision could she make? She didn't want him to go, but if he didn't the pain would only be worse when, inevitably, he left her for good.

'I don't know,' she said, swallowing a mouthful of pancake. 'I—I'll think about it.'

'Not for long, you won't,' he said, with such conviction that she knew he wanted to say more.

'No, I—no, not for long. Give me—give me the weekend.' She stared into the cup of tea he had placed in front of her and then said hesitantly, 'Max, it's Saturday. We can't stay alone here all day...'

'Driving each other crazy?' He dropped a knife on to his plate with a clatter. 'No, we can't. So what do you propose we do about it?'

'Well—we could go to the Hoh rain forest. It's a long drive.'

'Which would keep me gainfully employed with my hands safely on the wheel and off you. Is that the idea?'

'Something like that,' she admitted.

He laughed, a hard, abrasive laugh that made her wince. 'All right, you're on. I'm expecting a phone call from my accountants in London some time soon. We'll leave after that.'

'Fine. And tomorrow I'm having lunch with my family,' she added quickly.

'So am I.'

'You are?' Faith looked up, startled and not best pleased. 'You mean they know you're here?'

'Coming from a girl who was brought up in Caley Cove, that's a very odd question,' he remarked drily.

She smiled for the first time that morning. 'Yes, I guess it is. Mrs Gruber again, I suppose.'

'Probably. We had a chat on the stairway yesterday.'

'Mrs Gruber doesn't chat. She interrogates.'

'Precisely.'

Faith began to feel better. This wry, non-aggressive Max she could cope with. It was the sexy rake who caused her all the problems. If only he would stay like this...

For most of the day, greatly to her relief, he did. He took his call, which seemed to go on for some time, then they climbed into the car and spent the drive to Hoh discussing the scenery and their respective families.

It turned out that Max and his younger brother had spent a very happy childhood growing up in Scotland. His parents had been devoted both to each other and to their children. Max referred to them affectionately as the ideal couple.

And for him, of course, there had always been the lure of the mountains.

They stopped for lunch at an attractive lakeside hotel, and their unusual amity continued. Faith had no difficulty now in understanding what it was that had drawn her to Max in the first place. He was a relaxed and considerate companion when he chose to be, and surprisingly urbane for one who had spent half his life in the wilds. Above all, and again only when he wanted to, he knew how to make her laugh.

It was early afternoon by the time they arrived in the rain forest, where the warm sun filtering through the trees seemed to touch the lush greenery around them with an ageless magic. There was something primeval, unchanging, here beneath the branches of the old trees standing tall and stately amidst the ferns and wildflowers and toadstools.

For a short time Faith felt at peace. Then she noticed that as they walked side by side, not touching, along the level trail that led to the Hall of Mosses, Max became preoccupied, silent, the man with the elsewhere eyes she had met that first day on the beach.

They stopped beneath an archway formed by ghostly hangings of thick club moss which drooped from the trees around them like ancient robes. There was a warm, earthy smell in the air, but Faith knew it didn't fit the mood of the man beside her.

'What's the matter?' she asked, when Max hadn't said a word for several minutes. 'Your supply of human blood running low?'

'Mmm?' He looked at her as if he'd forgotten she existed. 'Nothing's the matter. And blood disagrees with my digestion.'

'Oh,' said Faith. 'Then what's with the air of gothic gloom?'

'The fact that I haven't chosen to talk for a whole three minutes doesn't mean I'm gloomy,' replied Max cuttingly. 'I suppose it didn't occur to you that I might just be enjoying all this timeless tranquillity?' He gestured at the forest around them as a soft breeze whispered through the leaves.

He didn't look as if he was enjoying anything very much, Faith thought. But he did look as if he belonged in this setting, surrounded by towering conifers and curtains of eerie green moss. Then, as the spicy scent of evergreens filled his nostrils, she felt a quick *frisson* of alarm.

'Do you mean you're feeling the call of the wild?' she asked lightly, careful to hide her dismay.

'Perhaps.' He ran his hand over the rough bark of a fir tree, not looking at her. 'In which case it's a call that won't be answered for a while. I imagine it will be June or July before my next expedition gets under way.'

'Oh.' Faith didn't want to think about June or July. Even if she made the decision he wanted, by that time Max would be gone. She still wasn't sure if she could bear to keep on loving him, and all the time live with the knowledge that soon that love would be no more than mist and a memory.

A pair of black-tail deer stepped daintily from the undergrowth at that moment, distracting her from her dismal forebodings of the future. As she and Max stood watching the shy creatures, who quickly disappeared into the bushes, for a while their easy camaraderie was restored.

Then, for no reason Faith could put her finger on, the atmosphere between them changed. Once more Max became taciturn and abstracted, and the drive home, although not hostile, was no longer relaxed and companionable. Both of them were lost in their own thoughts, and Faith sensed in him a subtle withdrawal, as if already he was preparing to depart.

Max, glancing at her cool and expressionless profile, wondered if he should do just that. It would be unadulterated hell to spend endless days and nights alone with Faith and be denied the ultimate intimacy. But if that was her decision, he must respect it. He had once thought, wrongly perhaps, that she would prove as foot-loose and fancy-free as himself. But somehow, when he hadn't been looking, he had a sense that something un-expected had happened.

He stared at the clouds looming on the horizon, thinking that, although he'd faced plenty of obstacles in his time, the Duchess here beside him could prove to be the greatest of them all.

Absorbed in these unsatisfactory reflections, he paid very little attention to anything except the road ahead of him until he happened to glance at the petrol gauge.

'Hell!' he muttered. 'I'll have to stop and fill up.'

Faith didn't answer. He looked tense, strained, as if any small aggravation might cause him to explode. And she doubted if anything she could say would help.

He pulled up to the first garage they came to, a two-pump affair on an isolated stretch of highway with no other buildings in sight.

A large woman in carpet slippers shuffled out. 'Can't help ya,' she puffed. 'Power's out. Can't work the pump.'

'Damn.' Max glanced at his watch. 'How far to the next gas station is it?'

'Port Angeles,' answered the woman laconically.

'But that's miles——'

'Yup. Power's bin out for three hours already. Some yahoo felled a tree on to a power pole, knocked out the whole area, he did.' She chuckled. 'One way to get out of a day's work.'

'I'd give him the whole damn year out,' muttered Max.

'When do you think you'll have power again?' asked Faith, smiling politely in an attempt to lessen the impact of Max's ill-humour.

''Bout an hour, maybe.'

'Can we get home on what we have?' she asked Max.

'No.'

She glanced dubiously at the rigid set of his jaw. 'Oh. Nothing we can do about it, then.' She made a valiant attempt to sound positive. 'It's not your fault.'

'Of course it's my fault. I should have checked the damn petrol. And don't be so bloody cheerful.'

He slammed his hand on the dashboard, and the woman in carpet slippers said blankly, 'What's he talking about, miss?'

'Petrol,' said Faith solemnly. 'Gas. I think he reverts to his native tongue when he's put out.'

'Oh,' said the woman, nodding sagely. 'Yeah, some of 'em do.'

Max swore quietly under his breath, and Faith realised his hold on his temper was even more fragile than she'd thought. Whatever had been eating at him on the way home wasn't going to be improved by an enforced wait at a garage whose proprietress was looking at him expectantly, as if she imagined he would break into some wild foreign war chant at any moment.

'Let's go for a walk,' she suggested. 'Just until the power comes back on.'

'Nowhere to walk,' said the woman. 'Bush is too thick around here. 'Less you want to walk along the highway. How about having a cup of tea instead?'

Max gave a derisive bark of laughter. 'Can't do anything right today, can I? Any teenager knows where to run out of *gas* in order to get his way with a girl. But I have to do it on a busy highway surrounded by impenetrable bush.'

'You're not a teenager,' Faith pointed out mildly.

'Darn right, he isn't,' said Carpet Slippers, glaring at Max as if she suspected he was quite capable of assault on a public highway. 'Better settle for the tea, miss, 'cos you sure aren't going nowhere till the power's on. *He...*' she tossed her head at Max '...can have some too. Hey!' As she leaned into the car, suddenly her pale, short-sighted eyes opened very wide. 'You. Seen you on TV, haven't I? You were talking about rescuing some guy from some mountain.'

'Failing to rescue,' said Max curtly. 'He died.'

'Yeah,' said the woman, 'that's right, I remember now. How about that!' She beamed at Max as if she had just been awarded a prize. 'That must have been real exciting.'

Faith took one look at Max's face and said quickly that they'd love some tea, thank you.

It was thick, black and bitter, and while they drank it its maker, delighted to have a captive celebrity, regaled them with tales of her nurse daughter in Seattle who was married to a car salesman whose mother had been married seven times. Max managed to endure it with stoical civility—out of habit, Faith supposed—but the look on his face grew bleaker by the moment, and she was casting about for a way to halt the flow, when suddenly the power came on. Max thanked their hostess with automatic good manners and hurried out to the pumps.

Faith heaved a sigh of relief, murmured her own thanks and hurried after him. A few minutes later they were once again speeding in grim silence down the road.

Max kept his eyes rigidly on the highway. It was dusk now, and the shadows were lengthening, falling across his face so she had no way of guessing what he was thinking. Earlier, she had assumed it was just physical frustration, and resentment at not getting his own way, that had caused him to go all grim and remote. But now she had a feeling there was more to it. Naturally he hadn't appreciated being reminded of his friend's 'exciting' death on a mountain, but his impatience with himself for running out of gas, and his irritation at the unavoidable delay, had been out of all proportion to its cause. It was almost as if he were looking for something, or someone, to lash out at—which wasn't like him.

He took the turn off the highway much too sharply. Faith jumped, and he tightened his grip on the wheel. 'It's getting late,' he said curtly. 'The Clambake is open again, isn't it? We'll eat there.'

'I've got food at home,' she protested.

'I dare say. But we're eating at the Clambake.'

'Why? Is there something wrong with my meals?' Max's brusque tone raised her hackles, made her feel belligerent.

'Not much that a good book of plain cooking wouldn't cure.' He spun the wheel, swung past her apartment block, and skimmed the car down the hill to the restaurant.

'Well, of all the rude, ungrateful...' Faith jerked round to deliver a blistering opinion of his manners face to face. But the words stopped at her lips.

Max was turned towards her, his arm along the back of the seat, and the look in his eyes was so implacable, so set, that she knew anything she said to him would be a waste of words.

She could, of course, tell him that, while *he* could do as he pleased, *she* was eating at home. But his knuckles were paper-white, clenched aggressively, and his body as it bent towards her was taut as strung out wire. She could tell he was forcing himself to stay in control. Of himself, obviously. She hoped he didn't have any plans to control her. In any case, there seemed no point in contributing to what looked like some kind of internal crisis. Especially as she suspected she *was* the crisis.

'All right,' she said calmly, 'we'll eat here if you like.' Then she couldn't resist adding, 'Perhaps tomorrow you'll find my mother's cooking more in keeping with your taste.'

'Hmm.' His eyes were hidden in the April twilight, but his skin seemed to have taken on a darker hue. Faith smiled inwardly, but without much lightening of her mood. That 'hmm' had been of the 'I'm sorry, but I'm damned if I'm going to admit it' variety. She was beginning to understand Max quite well.

They ate quickly, and afterwards Faith couldn't have said what she'd ordered. She was just thankful that there were only two other tables occupied, both of them by tourists passing through. All she needed right now was to have her strained and generally silent dinner with Max reported all over town as the beginning of the romance that wasn't.

The moment they got back to her apartment she hurried into the kitchen to make tea and coffee. Max muttered something sarcastic to the effect that he supposed she was planning another evening of riveting TV, and went to the coat cupboard to fetch a folder crammed with papers and brochures.

When Faith came back, she discovered him sitting on the floor surrounded by maps, charts and intimidating pages of figures.

'Oh, you're working,' she remarked unnecessarily.

'Yes, I do sometimes. Since coming here, not nearly as much as I expected.' He didn't look up, but continued to make notes with a silver pencil.

Faith eyed his bent head reflectively. It was possible he really wanted to work, although he'd had several uninterrupted days already in which to complete what needed to be done. More likely he was putting her in her place.

She switched the TV on, looking for a reaction which didn't come. Max went on writing, so she sat down to watch a programme on ostrich farming.

After a while he looked up long enough to remark that ostriches certainly fitted the occasion, and Faith said, 'I'm going to bed.'

'Good.' He put down the pencil and stretched. 'Is that your decision?'

'Yes—I mean, no. I mean——'

'You mean you're planning to continue your campaign to drive me crazy,' he interrupted. 'OK, two can play at that game.'

She was curled up on a cushion only a foot away from where he lounged against the wall with his legs stretched comfortably in front of him. Without giving her time to think, Max pushed his papers out of the way, put his arms around her and pulled her on to his thighs.

'That's better,' he said, settling her more firmly. 'Now, if I remember correctly, this ought to have the desired effect.'

She gasped as he slipped a hand inside the waistband of her jeans and splayed his fingers out, sending a soft, erotic message up her spine. With his other hand he began to stroke the back of her neck. When she moaned, he pulled her lips against his, kissed her with agonising thoroughness and let her go.

She didn't move, but sat there, dazed, staring into his eyes, so he put both hands on her waist and tipped her back on to the cushions. 'There,' he said, 'I believe that's that bit of business taken care of. Goodnight, Faith. I hope you sleep as well as I probably won't.'

'Bastard.' Faith stood up, trying to look dignified, but as her hair was hanging in tangles across her face, and she could feel a deep flush warming her cheeks, she hadn't much hope that she'd succeeded.

'Thank you,' said Max politely. 'That's one of the nicer names I've been called.'

She could well believe it. She turned her back on him, opened the bedroom door and prepared to slam it, only just remembering in time that Mrs Gruber and her broom were on the warpath.

Behind her, Max drew a hand across his eyes and gazed with stony concentration at a map of Chile.

'Where are Mom and Dad?' asked Faith the next day, when Bruce opened the door to her and Max.

'Dad's in the living-room conducting two chairs and the coffee table,' said Bruce with cheerful and surprising tolerance. 'Mom's on the phone trying to convince Mrs Bracken that you and Max aren't actually engaged.'

Faith could almost feel Max stiffen, although he wasn't touching her and she couldn't see his face. 'Oh. Well, let's—let's go and sit down. Interrupt Dad's opera,' she said brightly, hoping Max's perceptive gaze wasn't on the flaming scarlet of her neck. The morning alone with him had been strained enough as it was.

Frank Farraday did indeed appear to be conducting the furniture. His thumb and forefinger were pressed together to form an imaginary baton, and his right arm was slicing vigorously through the air.

'*Turandot* still?' enquired Faith, more for something to say than because she wanted to irritate her father.

Frank jumped, cleared his throat. 'Nope. Callas in *Butterfly*. I can hear the music in my head.' He looked defensively at Max over Faith's shoulder.

'My father used to do the same thing,' said Max. 'He said he found it relaxing.'

Frank beamed, and once again Faith found herself resenting Max's knack for putting everyone except herself at ease.

She left the two of them discussing *Madam Butterfly* and went to see if her mother had succeeded in squashing the rumours.

She hadn't.

Jane was just hanging up the phone. 'Molly says you're planning on a June wedding,' she said, the moment Faith entered the kitchen. 'I told her you weren't, but she said she had it first hand from the Clambake——'

'Max won't even be here in June,' Faith cut her mother off wearily. 'And we're not planning any kind of wedding.'

Jane frowned. 'Oh. One of these modern arrangements. Faith, I really don't think——'

'No, not any kind of arrangement. Max is leaving. He's going back to his beloved mountains.'

Jane groped in the pocket of her apron and pulled out a pair of steel glasses. 'Oh,' she said, scrutinising her daughter more closely. And then, 'He's taking advantage of you, isn't he?' She began to stir a pot on the stove.

'No,' said Faith, 'he isn't.'

'Hmm. He strikes me as the sort of man who knows what he wants and goes after it.'

'Yes, I suppose he is.'

'And he wants you, doesn't he? I can recognise forked lightning when I see it.'

Faith adjusted the sash on her blue and white polka-dotted jumpsuit. 'Yes,' she agreed, 'he does.'

'Faith...' Her mother swung round, spilling gravy on to the element. 'Faith, do be careful. I don't want to see you get hurt.'

'I won't be. Don't worry.'

It wasn't really a lie. She wouldn't be because she already was.

Jane sighed and turned back to what was left of the gravy.

Lunch, like last night's dinner, was strained, mainly because Jane made no effort to conceal that she'd crossed Max's name from her list of contenders in the son-in-law stakes.

'Would you care for some pie, Mr Kain?' she asked at the end of the meal, looking down her nose at Max and managing to indicate that she thought he'd had more than enough already.

'Yes, please,' said Max, 'I'd love some.'

Faith folded her napkin and stole a quick glance at his face. It expressed nothing but innocent appreciation of Jane's cooking, but she didn't believe for a moment that he was unaware of the currents of disapproval emanating from her mother's end of the table.

They left soon after lunch because Faith couldn't stand the atmosphere any longer. She explained that she had a lot of housework to catch up on.

'What housework?' asked Max as he helped her into the car. 'Planning to rearrange the cushions, are you?'

'No.' Faith snapped her seatbelt into place with a vicious click. 'I have a problem with house pests. I'm thinking of getting busy with the bug spray.'

'Ouch,' said Max. 'I *am* unpopular with the Farraday ladies today. And I thought I was being particularly charming.'

'Hah, so you did notice.'

'Notice what?'

'My mother.'

'Ah. Yes, I've traversed quite a few icefields in my time, but today was the first time I've ever felt in danger of ending up in the family deep-freeze.' He smoothed a hand over his jaw. 'By the way, which of your unlucky ex-suitors did we have for lunch? He was very tasty.'

Faith choked, tried to keep a straight face, and failed totally.

'Stephen?' suggested Max, when she didn't answer. 'I wouldn't mind getting my teeth into him.'

She unclasped her seatbelt and collapsed against the dashboard, shoulders shaking. 'No,' she managed to gasp out. 'Mother never liked Stephen. I'm sure she wouldn't want him in her freezer.'

'Mmm, a relief on the whole,' he murmured, lifting her hair and stroking it over her shoulder.

Faith, who had been struggling to sit up, collapsed again, until Max, with a resigned sigh, pulled her up-right and refastened her seatbelt.

'I'm glad to see you've recovered your good humour,' he said drily. 'Where to? Home to collect the bug spray, I presume.'

'Yes, that will do nicely,' she said primly. 'And speaking of humour, yours hasn't been up to much lately.'

'I know.'

No apology, just a quiet acknowledgement of fact. But the touch of his fingers had brought her swiftly back to the realisation that Max's ability to make her laugh had in no way solved the problems between them, or helped her make the decision she expected him to demand at any moment.

Only it wasn't a decision he demanded after they had climbed the stairs up to her apartment. It was an explanation.

'Your mother,' he said, taking Faith firmly by the elbows. 'What have I done?'

She stared at the warm brown of his sweater where it circled the sinews of his neck and thought of his behaviour of the night before, for which he'd offered no explanation. 'Do you care?' she asked tartly. 'Or is it just that you can't take it when someone fails to treat you like a conquering hero?'

His grip tightened a fraction. 'If that bothered me, I wouldn't be here, Duchess.'

She thought about that and decided that as usual he was right. Hero-worship wasn't part of her make-up. Especially when the hero was a sexy, arrogant man of the mountains called Max.

'Mother's worried,' she said, her attention still fixed on his neck.

'Yes, that was the impression I formed. Why? Does she think I'm likely to ravish you—and leave you alone, penniless and pregnant?'

'I expect it's crossed her mind. Except that she knows I wouldn't allow it.'

'Then what's worrying her?' Max moved his hands up her arms. 'And why won't you look at me?'

Faith made an effort and raised her eyes as far as his chin, which looked very square and aggressive. 'She's worried about *me*,' she said, in a voice so low that Max could barely hear it.

'I *had* figured that much out. But if she doesn't have me cast as the villain of a Victorian melodrama, what in hell does she imagine I can do to you?'

Indignation began to replace embarrassment, and Faith lifted her chin and glared straight into his eyes. 'I have feelings, in case you haven't noticed. Mother's afraid they'll be hurt.'

'Hmm.' He let her go, and it was as if a mask had dropped over his face as he moved away from her to stand with his back to the window. 'And will they?'

Dear God, he really doesn't know, Faith thought despairingly. She gazed at him, standing straight and arrogant with his palms pressed behind him on the sill. His features were set, uncompromising, and the sun shining on his hair was turning it to burning copper. He looked a picture of almost godlike masculinity—and of course he *wouldn't* know. He was, as her mother had said, a man who went after what he wanted, and once he had it he moved on to the next challenge. It probably never occurred to him that other people had needs that were very different from his own.

She saw that his dark eyebrows were drawn down now and that he was studying her with a peculiar intensity. As if I'm a specimen in a lab, she thought, drawing herself up to her full height.

'Not at all,' she said, in her best bored Duchess voice. 'Why should they be?'

'I've no idea.' He swung round to stare through the window, and something about the way he held his shoulders made her frown. She wondered, just briefly, if perhaps he wasn't as oblivious to her needs as she'd thought. Then he pivoted on his heel again and strode across to the door.

'I need some air,' he said shortly. 'You can forget the bug spray.'

Before she could form a response the door had slammed closed behind him and Mrs Gruber was pounding on the ceiling.

Faith, who normally ignored her eccentric neighbour, lifted a blue-sandalled foot and stamped back. When that didn't make enough noise, she grabbed her banjo and began to play *Pop Goes the Weasel*. Over and over again until her frustration had worked itself out. By that time Mrs Gruber's fist was banging on her door.

'Sorry, Mrs Gruber,' she called. 'It won't happen again.'

'Huh. Gone for good, has he?' Her cantankerous neighbour's voice was filled with vindictive satisfaction, and a moment later Faith heard her stomping down the stairs to spread the news all over Caley Cove.

But Max hadn't gone for good. He came back just as Faith was finishing a supper of scrambled eggs and cheese, and after greeting her curtly he sat down at once against the wall.

'Have you eaten?' she asked, following him into the living-room.

'Mm-hm. At the Clambake.' He picked up a leather-bound notebook and his silver pencil.

All right, thought Faith, so that's how it's going to be, is it?

She left him to his silent contemplation of a blank page, and started to load dishes into the sink. When she was finished she pulled Plato's *Symposium* from behind the breadbin and announced that she was going to read in bed.

Max glanced at the title of her book, muttered something about it matching his mood, and growled an offhand goodnight.

As she stared dully at the pages that until today had never failed to absorb her, Faith heard Max switch the TV on to something that sounded as though Godzilla had just encountered King Kong.

She presumed that also matched his mood.

He was still asleep, or pretending to be, when she tiptoed out of the apartment on Monday morning.

When she came home that evening, he was gone.

CHAPTER EIGHT

AT FIRST Faith was too busy backing an armload of groceries through the door to notice that Max wasn't there. But when no pair of healthy masculine arms materialised to relieve her of her burden, she dumped the grocery bags on to the counter and glanced around.

No sign of Max. And both the bedroom and the bathroom were empty.

When there was still no sign of him by seven o'clock, she gave a sigh of exasperation, decided he wasn't worth starving for, and for the second night in a row sat down alone to scrambled eggs. 'Honestly,' she muttered to the empty chair across from her, 'you might at least have had the courtesy to leave a note.'

The chair wasn't responsive, and by the time eleven o'clock rolled around exasperation began to turn to worry.

For the first time since she'd come home, it occurred to Faith to see if Max's bag and papers were still taking up space in her coat cupboard.

They weren't. She stared vacantly at the empty space on the floor, and at the shoes piled up to one side. He had gone. For good, presumably. Just plain up and gone, without even saying goodbye. Or thank you. Or thanks for the memories. Or anything. Just—gone.

Slowly, her feet dragging, Faith wandered out to the kitchen, slumped on to a chair beside the table, and buried her face in her hands.

She felt the muscles round her eyes start to constrict. No. No, she was not going to cry. She'd cried enough tears over Stephen, who hadn't been worth it. Max, it seemed, was no different. He had loved her and left her, and she had no one to blame but herself. He had made no promises, and her confidence that he wouldn't just leave when the spirit moved him had been naïve. And stupid—unbelievably stupid.

Biting her lip, Faith stood up. All right, so for the second time in her life she had made a big mistake. It was a mistake she would never make again. And what she had to do now was find some way of getting through the night.

She pulled out the paint cans she'd been saving for just the right moment, and painted the whole apartment eggshell-white.

At four o'clock in the morning she went to bed.

'Now what?'

Faith looked up from her computer to meet Angela's perceptive glare. She blinked. 'What do you mean?'

'You look as though you've slept all of five minutes, you're wearing a face like an uncooked pancake—and that Flanders Field dress again.'

'Oh.' Faith glanced down and realised that her boss was right. 'Sorry.'

'Never mind sorry. What's the matter? I don't know what it is about this office, but it has a very odd effect on my secretaries. First Sarah, and now you.'

'What?' Faith blinked again.

'Look, I may be very happily divorced, but if you think I don't know lovestruck when I see it, you're dead wrong.' Angela frowned severely. 'It's getting to be a positive plague.'

Faith picked up a pencil, started to chew it, and discovered she was munching the point. She laid it back on her blotter. 'Max has gone.'

'Yes, I know. He's gone to Seattle with your brother. I heard Bruce is signing up for some courses there and looking for somewhere to stay. About time, if you ask me.'

'What?' Faith rubbed her ear. 'Angela, how do you know that?'

'Your mother told Molly Bracken, who told Doris at the post office, who——'

Faith held up her hand. 'OK. For a moment I forgot I was back in Caley Cove.' She swung her chair away from the computer and stared without seeing it at a row of books on legal history. 'I guess my mother thought I already knew.'

Angela folded her arms and propped herself up against the wall. 'He's coming back, isn't he?'

'No,' said Faith, 'he's not coming back. His bag and papers are gone, and he didn't even tell me he was leaving.'

'Bastard,' said Angela succinctly.

Faith wanted to agree with her, but somehow she couldn't. Max had left her in the cruellest way possible, but he hadn't really meant to be cruel. He had warned her he would go, and he'd gone. Their relationship had been short, volatile and, for a few hours, unbearably sweet. Exactly the sort of relationship he wanted. She had thought for a while it might be what she wanted too.

Only it hadn't been.

That evening, as Faith trailed tiredly up the road from the beach carrying her banjo, she couldn't help hoping that by some miracle she'd got it all wrong—that when she got home Max would be standing in her living-room wearing his powerhouse suit and demanding to take her out to dinner.

But he wasn't, and although she told herself it was a good thing, that she'd be much better off without him, she knew she didn't really believe it.

By the following morning, when she stumbled bleary-eyed and exhausted into the kitchen after a sleepless night, she was too weary and dejected to believe in anything. Even the presence of a very presentable male backside protruding from the cupboard beneath her sink failed to rouse her from her apathy and depression. Obviously it had to be a delusion brought on by an acute lack of sleep.

She turned away, went to put the kettle on without filling it, and sniffed vaguely at a faint smell of smoke. Mrs Gruber burning her toast again, presumably. When she heard something metallic clatter on to the floor behind her, she paid no attention. But when the clatter was followed by an ear-bending string of curses, it was slowly borne in on her that she'd heard some of those colourful variations on the English language before. And there was nothing delusional about them, or about the voice that appeared to be carrying on a furious conversation with the underside of her sink.

Faith gulped, put a hand to her mouth and stepped backwards. 'Max...?' she began, still not quite able to comprehend that the firm thighs spread across her floor, and the familiarly delectable backside, were actually real. 'Max...?'

A pair of jeans-clad legs shifted slightly. 'Damn it, Faith,' the voice roared up at her, 'don't you know enough not to store paint rags in an enclosed space?'

Paint rags? Faith's mouth fell open. After a two-day absence, during which she had missed him quite desperately, Max had come back to her. And all he could do was swear at her about paint rags? She felt an odd sort of lump in her throat, not sure if she wanted to laugh or cry. Then Max swore again, and she stopped feeling as if this whole insane drama was a dream that wasn't really happening, and came down to earth with a thud.

'Where I store my property is my business,' she said tightly. 'Can't *you* even be bothered to let me know when you're coming or going? This isn't a flophouse for indigent tourists who climb mountains. Nor is it a bed-and-breakfast.'

'No, it's a fire-trap.'

Faith took a deep breath and found it didn't help much. Then she cast a retaliatory eye over the vulnerable parts of Max that added such an improving dimension to her floor. Deliberately, she lifted a foot.

'Don't try it,' he growled.

'Try what?'

'Biting the hand that puts out the fires caused by your stupidity.'

Faith curled her fingers tightly into her palms. 'What fires? And I was thinking of kicking, if you must know.'

'That's what I thought. Like I said, don't try it. I'm talking about the fire under your sink, woman. The one I arrived just in time to put out.' He twisted his body sideways, and dumped a metal bowl filled with the charred remains of paint rags at her feet. Reluctantly she lowered her foot. There wasn't much point in attacking him while he was in the middle of extinguishing a fire caused, as he had quite rightly and very rudely said, by her own stupidity.

Besides, she had a feeling Max wasn't the kind of man who would take an assault on his personal parts without briskly returning the favour.

A moment later he eased himself out of the cupboard. 'Get rid of this,' he ordered from the floor, pointing at the bowl and its unappetising contents.

With an effort Faith managed not to close his peremptory mouth with her bare foot. She had an idea that if she did she would find the bowl summarily upended on her head. Max, with his thick brown hair dusty white, and his hands and cream sports shirt soot-covered, did not look in an accommodating mood.

She picked up the bowl without a word and carried it obediently into the bathroom. When she came back she found Max running water into the sink and over his head.

'There's a shower in the bathroom,' she pointed out.

'Later.' He turned the tap off and straightened, his grey gaze moving almost insultingly over her slender figure. She was wearing a mauve cotton nightgown, and because it was a warm, sunny morning she hadn't bothered to put on a robe.

'Is that all the thanks I get?' he asked, when he had finished a leisurely appraisal.

'Thanks for what?' Faith tossed her head back and glowered. 'For treating me like an underpaid housekeeper?'

'Some housekeeper.' He gestured at the sooty shambles beneath her sink, then cast a disparaging eye at an untidy pile of cushions that partially blocked the entrance to the kitchen. When she continued to glower, he added grimly, 'As a matter of fact, my dear Duchess, I was anticipating a properly grateful reward for preventing what could have been a serious fire.'

'I'd have smelled it myself and put it out,' said Faith, who wasn't sure what she felt at this moment, except that it wasn't gratitude. Nor had a minor fire in her kitchen anything to do with the conflicting messages her body was sending to her brain. She wanted to throw her arms around Max, soot and all, as he lounged with a hip propped against the edge of the counter and water glistening attractively in his hair. She also wanted to hit him. 'Max,' she continued tightly, 'I've spent two days missing you and worrying about you and wondering why you left so suddenly. And you had no right to let yourself into my apartment and my life again and turn up under my sink.'

'I'm sorry for saving you and Mrs Gruber from a fiery fate,' said Max, curling his lip. When he saw Faith open her mouth to deliver another blistering attack, he added, 'And the fact of the matter is that you *didn't* smell it burning. I've been driving half the night, Faith, and, believe me, it didn't do a thing for my disposition to find your kitchen filling up with smoke. Damn it, woman...' he glared at her and she saw him clench his fists '...don't you realise that if I hadn't arrived when I did you could have been killed?'

'I would have smelled it,' repeated Faith. She could understand his anger, but her disposition wasn't up to much this morning either. 'Max, what is it about you that attracts fires?' She thrust out her chin, picked up the kettle again and squeezed past him, taking care not to brush against his leg.

When she turned on the tap, at once, and very firmly, the kettle was taken out of her hand. 'That's enough,' said Max, putting his hands on her shoulders and spinning her round to face him. 'Now say thank you. And promise me you'll never do such an idiotic thing again.'

Faith felt a little guilty. He *had* put out the fire caused entirely by her own carelessness. She did know better. On the other hand, she wouldn't have been careless if her brain hadn't been put on idle by his abrupt departure...

'I promise. And thank you,' she said woodenly.

Max shook his head, and brushed a hand through his already disordered hair. 'All right, I suppose that will have to do for the moment. But I won't put up with your Duchess act this morning, madam. So cut it out, will you? We have to talk.'

'What's to talk about?' asked Faith. 'Couldn't you find a suitable bed-and-breakfast?' She laid special emphasis on the 'bed', then added, 'Why didn't you ask Nellie McNaughton? She might be willing to give up Ted.'

'Faith——'

'And in any case, I'm not open for business,' she said coldly.

'Faith, for Pete's sake...' He paused, drew a deep breath. 'Listen, I know you're upset, but——'

'But I'm supposed to forget that you walked out on me without a word, and invite you to take up residence again. Is that it?'

Something dangerous flared in his eyes, but Faith was too overwrought to care.

'Look,' he said, tightening his hold on her arms, 'you're angry——'

'Yes, I am,' she interrupted. 'Shouldn't I be?'

'I suppose so, only——'

'Only you want me to kiss and make up. So you'll have another chance to kiss and run?'

'Right,' said Max, 'that does it.'

Before she had a chance to protest, he had swept one arm around her waist, and the knuckles of his free hand were tilting up her chin. He glared down at her for a moment, making her heart jump crazily, then bent his head and covered her mouth fiercely with his lips.

She started to pull away, but his kiss deepened, sent an immediate and drugging need seething through her blood as he slid his hands down her hips and trapped her right leg firmly between his thighs. She no longer wanted him to stop. Then for a split second he drew his head back, and she saw his eyes, deep, smoky, reflecting something that almost gave her hope. Resistance evaporated. She knew what she wanted now, and she took it, dust, soot-covered shirt and all.

Linking her arms round his neck, she pulled his face down to hers and kissed him—a long, lingering, melting kiss that at the back of what was left of her mind she knew could only lead to one thing.

But it didn't, because abruptly Max drew back, unclasped her arms, and muttered half to himself, 'Hell, I didn't mean to do that, Duchess.'

'Didn't you?' said Faith shakily.

'What?' He ran a hand over his hair and it came away wet. 'No, I most certainly did not. All the same, I'm sorely tempted to do it again. Except that I've already made enough mess of your nightgown.' His voice altered, became rougher. 'And not just your nightgown either.'

'Have you?' Faith glanced down and saw that the mauve gown was indeed splotched with ugly black soot. 'Don't worry,' she shrugged, 'it'll wash out.'

Max didn't answer, and Faith's eyebrows drew together in a puzzled frown.

He was looking at her with the strangest expression she'd ever seen. His eyes seemed darker and deeper than usual, and they were fixed on her face as if he were a condemned man looking his last on the world—which was a ridiculous flight of morbid fancy. She shook her head, bewildered and unsure of what was happening. 'Max,' she whispered at last. 'Max, I don't understand.'

'No, I don't expect you to.'

'Oh.' She put her hands behind her back and tried not to show that she was hurt by his aloofness. 'All right, but would you please tell me what's going on? Why did you leave without saying anything? What brought you back? And why did you make me kiss you—and then pretend you didn't mean to do it?'

'I wasn't pretending.'

'Oh? Then whose were those arms around me? Whose lips can I still taste on my tongue?'

'Listen.' Max took a quick step towards her, then thought better of it and hitched his hip on a corner of the table.

'I am listening.'

'Good. First of all, I left without telling you because I thought that as long as you were mad at me you weren't likely to miss me too much——'

'No problem,' said Faith acidly. 'I didn't.' Lord, what had made her say that? He knew it wasn't true. She'd missed him desperately.

'Thank you. Secondly, I came back because I couldn't do anything else. When Bruce asked me to take him to Seattle, I agreed because I needed time away from you to think...'

'Very enlightening. And how do you explain the kiss that wasn't meant to happen?'

Max folded his arms on his chest, and the look he gave her made her think of winter and cold grey sleet. 'Don't push me, Faith. I'm not in any mood to take it.'

'And I'm not in any mood to take a load of self-serving baloney from you.' She stared over his shoulder, avoiding his wintry glare, and at once her gaze fell on the clock. Her eyes widened. 'Apart from which, I'm due at work in less than an hour, so can we postpone this fascinating discussion until later? Assuming you're planning to stay in town.' She flung around to pull the kettle off the stove and throw a teabag into a cup.

'I'm not—or not for long. But I'll be here when you get home from work.' His tone was so bleak that Faith was briefly distracted from making the tea which was all she'd have time for this morning.

When she looked at him she saw that his mouth was drawn into a straight line and the muscles of his face were pulled tight. The knuckles of one hand gripped the edge of the table, and, in spite of her determination not to let him see that she was hurting, she shivered slightly.

'You haven't eaten,' said Max, as she picked up her cup and started to make for the bedroom.

'I haven't time.'

'Then make time.'

She spun round, nearly spilling the tea. 'Don't tell me what to do, Max. *You're* the reason I'm late.' Without waiting for his answer, she swung away again.

To her surprised relief, he didn't try to stop her.

But when she hurried into the kitchen ten minutes later and dumped her cup into the sink, he was behind her at once and she felt two strong hands grab her by the elbows. Before she had time to remonstrate, she found herself pulled backwards and pressed down into a chair.

'Toast,' said Max tersely, waving at a plate on the table. 'Eat it.'

'I told you, I haven't time——'

'I don't care whether you've got time or not. Do as you're told. I'll phone your boss for you.'

'You,' said Faith through her teeth, 'are *not* my boss, and——'

But Max, paying no attention to her, was already dialling. She heard him explain to Angela that her secretary would be a little late but that *he* was entirely to blame. Then after a short pause he smiled and hung up the phone with a clipped, 'Thank you. I was sure you'd agree.'

'There,' he said with maddening assurance, 'that's taken care of. Why aren't you eating?'

'Because I'm still gritting my teeth.'

'Well, don't. Use them on your toast.'

Faith glowered at him. 'You, Max Kain, can count yourself lucky I'm not using them on you.'

'Why? Because I've made you take time for breakfast? Since when has that been a crime?'

She brushed a hand over her eyes. Her limbs felt heavy, and suddenly she was so weary she wondered how she

would ever make it to work. 'No,' she said, 'I've just
realised breakfast has nothing to do with it.'

'I didn't think it had.' Max sounded weary too. 'Eat
your toast, Faith. We can talk later.'

She ate the toast.

Because it was unusually busy at work that day, she
didn't have much time to brood over Max's inexplicable
behaviour. She was glad of that, because every now and
then, in the few minutes of respite between urgent jobs,
she remembered the hollow harshness of his voice when
he'd told her he didn't plan to stay in town. She didn't
want to think about that. She didn't want to think about
anything. Thinking and feeling were too painful.

But when five o'clock came Faith knew she had to
make a decision. She could go home and face whatever
was coming, or she could put the future on hold for a
while, go to the beach, and let the warm sun and the
timelessness of the waves wash away some of her doubt
and tension.

The seductive pull of the sea was hard to resist, but
in the end she forced herself to return to the apartment.
If Max was leaving, as he had promised, she might as
well tell him to go at once and get the agony over.

Reluctantly she dragged her feet up the stairs past Mrs
Gruber's partially opened door, her footsteps becoming
slower and slower. By the time she reached the top step
she was scarcely moving at all.

The door to her apartment opened suddenly and Max
was there, looming over her.

'What the hell kept you?' he demanded. 'I saw you
turn into the driveway.'

Faith looked up, saw that his eyes were as bleak as
ever, and lowered her head. 'I don't know,' she said list-

lessly. 'What's to hurry for? There's no... Oh, I see. Are you leaving, then? Now?'

He reached for her wrist and pulled her up beside him. 'I don't think so. I have to talk to you first.'

'Why? What about?' Faith couldn't see the point of talking any more, and the feel of him at her side, the subtle scent of his body, was both an aphrodisiac and a wound in her heart.

'Us.' His tone was so remote that she felt not even the faintest whisper of hope as he marched her into the apartment and closed the door. He was wearing black now, black jeans, black sweatshirt. She wondered if his choice of clothes was deliberate.

He held on to her wrist as he kicked aside a cushion and led her into the kitchen. Faith wasn't altogether surprised to see that another of Bodger's concoctions was already served up and steaming on the table.

'Eat first. Then we'll talk.' He gestured at the food, the rough edge of his voice holding out no hope that he would say anything she wanted to hear.

Faith ate the food without tasting it. She had a vague idea that by some miracle it might give her much needed courage to cope with whatever was coming.

In fact, all it gave her was a headache.

When she sat down after clearing the table, Max took the chair across from her and said quietly, 'Faith, you and I have to get a few things straight.'

'Do we?' she asked without much interest. 'I don't see why.'

Something that was more than impatience and less than pain flared in his eyes very briefly. Then he placed both fists on the table, leaned towards her and said, 'Because I don't believe in unfinished business.'

'Don't you? What business?' Faith couldn't really bring herself to care. Whatever he said, nothing between them would change. She stared at his tough forearms resting on the table, and noticed that all the veins in them stood out.

'Faith . . .' Max closed his eyes, started again. 'You're in love with me, aren't you?' He spoke with a desperate weariness that made her want to take him in her arms. But she couldn't do that. He didn't want her.

Gradually her incomprehensible urge to comfort this arrogant, unbearably beautiful man who was sitting at her kitchen table accusing her of undying devotion turned into empty despair. Because Max spoke the truth. She did love him. And it was hopeless.

'Yes,' she said, gazing at a burn mark on the table, 'I suppose I am. I seem to have a talent for picking unsuitable men.'

He made a sound that she'd never heard before. It wasn't quite a groan, but it seemed to come from deep inside his throat.

'Faith,' he said, in a voice she scarcely recognised, 'don't make this more difficult than it has to be.'

'Difficult for whom?' she asked coldly. 'You, I suppose.'

She was still staring at the burn mark, so she didn't see his hand snaking across the table until it already had hold of her wrist. 'Don't, Faith,' he said harshly.

For a moment she felt a flicker of surprise because his voice still had that odd, cracked sound. Then she decided she must have imagined it as he went on brusquely, 'I'm sorry. I didn't mean this to happen.'

'What didn't you mean to happen?'

'Don't you know?' Max's eyes narrowed disbelievingly. 'I told myself all along that you wanted the same thing I wanted—a pleasantly casual intimacy that would end the day I left town. I should have known better.' He released her and bowed his head on his hands.

'Should you?' said Faith heavily. 'I don't see why. You told me right from the start that you didn't want a permanent arrangement. You were always honest with me, Max. And in case you wondered, I didn't intend to be one of the lucky ladies you loved and left behind you either.' She shrugged. 'But as usual you got what you wanted.'

He was silent for a moment, then he lifted his head and said abruptly, 'I suppose I did. What I asked for, anyway.'

'It must be nice.'

'What must?'

'Always to get what you want.'

He frowned, but his reply, when it came, sounded hoarse, as though it were being dragged from him by force. 'Not always. Sometimes you get a hell of a lot more than you bargained for, believe me.'

Faith looked up then, thinking that behind the harsh words she heard a faint echo of truth. But his face was as inscrutable as a rock, impossible to read or to crack. 'Max,' she said, deciding she could take no more of this painfully enigmatic conversation. 'Max, I do love you. I don't want to, but I can't help it. If there's something you must say to me, please say it. If not, please just go.'

He picked up her hand, stared down at it, then dropped it abruptly and stood up. 'You're right,' he said, his fists pressed against the table as he bent over her.

'That's exactly what I have to say, Faith. I am leaving. But this time I won't be coming back to——'

'To put out my fires?' she interrupted, with a high, brittle laugh that even to her own ears sounded as though it verged on hysteria. 'Oh, dear, however will I manage?'

'Cut it out, Faith.' Max spoke brutally, slicing through her self-protective derision. But when she raised her head to dash an irritating moisture from her eyes, she saw that there was more than just impatience in the hard look that met her wounded gaze. He looked gaunt, hollow-eyed and very tired.

'Why did you come back?' she asked, making an effort to keep her voice steady.

To her astonishment, he smiled, but it was a bitter, twisted smile that didn't get anywhere near his eyes. 'I told you, I went away because I needed time to think.' He paused, and when he spoke again his voice had deepened. 'I came back because I had to say goodbye.'

Faith heard him, but refused to let the words penetrate. 'What did you need to think about?' she asked, once again staring at the table. The burn mark had assumed the shape of a bat.

'About what I'd done—to you. About what I was going to do in the future.'

'Oh. Really? And what *are* you going to do to me in the future?'

'Nothing. I'm going back to Seattle.'

Just like that. All at once, Faith's unusual apathy dropped away and emotions began to pour out of her like water surging over a dam.

'Oh, are you?' she cried, shoving her chair back and leaping to her feet. 'So the lord and master has had his way with the foolish virgin——'

'The foolish *what*?' he interrupted.

'Figure of speech,' she grated. 'And just because Stephen and I ... I mean, we were going to get married. That didn't make me fair game for——'

'Faith, I didn't say it did.'

'No, but you thought it. And now silly little me has gone and fallen in love with you, and that doesn't sit quite well with your conscience, does it, Mr Heroic Conqueror of Mountains? So you're running away before I become too inconvenient, and before you have to face the fact that you're nothing but a low-down, dirty——'

'Faith! That's enough.' He caught her by the shoulders, his eyes blazing with more than affronted male pride, and just for a moment she was afraid of him. 'I'm not running away, you dim-witted, beautiful imbecile. I'm leaving because I've hurt you enough, and it's time I got out of your hair and let you get on with your life. Don't you understand that I deliberately took off with Bruce without telling you because I wanted you to know me for what I am? Don't you have the brains to see that I can't ever give you what you need? What you deserve? I'm not leaving because you're inconvenient, you idiotic woman.' His features, which had been contorted by an exasperated kind of frustration, smoothed out then so that only his eyes seemed alive.

'Damn it, Faith,' he finished in a voice so deep with pain she could scarcely hear it. 'Damn it, Faith, I don't just want you. I love you.'

CHAPTER NINE

THE joy reflected in Faith's eyes beamed out at Max like violets opening to the sun. Then doubt, slowly returning, crept over her face softly as a cloud.

He watched her, unsmiling, and when she said nothing, only gazed up at him with those big, clouded eyes, he dropped his hands from her shoulders and went to stare out of the window.

A trace of snow still remained on the furthest mountains, and in that moment he wished with a ferocious intensity that he was out there where the air was pure and cold, pushing himself to the limits of endurance until his mind was addled by fatigue and exhaustion, instead of here, in this room, breaking the heart of the only woman he had ever allowed himself to love. Breaking it with ruthless resolution. Because he had to.

Faith's voice, low and unhappy, followed him across the room. He guessed she was finding it difficult to speak.

'Max...? Max, if you love me, why are you leaving? And why didn't you tell me before? About—about loving me?'

'How could I?' he rasped. 'I didn't know. Or if I did, I wouldn't admit it. When I finally faced the reality, I went away—to get my feelings in some sort of perspective. Your feelings too. Dear God, Faith, I never meant to hurt you.' He pressed his head against the cold glass of the window, and went on in a voice harsh with regret, 'If you want the truth, I'm not sure I should have told you even now. It doesn't change anything. I came back to say goodbye, not to raise any false hopes.'

'False—but why? Why, Max? I don't understand.'

He could hear the hurt in her voice and he closed his eyes. 'Faith—Duchess—don't you see? I'll never marry you, or anyone. I told you before, I'm not the rose-covered cottage type. You need someone who can give you what you deserve.'

'And what's that?'

He heard the beginnings of anger now. The fury of a woman scorned? He lifted his head and fixed his gaze on the mountains. 'You deserve a home, a family, and a man who doesn't risk his neck as a way of life. A man who'll love you and cherish you—who'll be there for you when you need him, share the good times as well as the bad. Help you raise your children. All the things that go to make a marriage. I can't give you those things, Faith——'

'You mean you won't.'

Faith couldn't hide her pain, or a hostility that threatened to choke her. She knew it made no sense, that there was no point in venting her anger on this man who said he loved her, and yet refused to yield any part of himself to make her happy. Refused even to consider the possibility that perhaps they could find a way to build a life together. But whether it made sense or not, she wanted to lash out, to wound him as he was wounding her...

She was so lost in her own misery that it was a moment before she realised he no longer had his back to her. Then he was across the kitchen in two strides, reaching for her.

Without stopping to think, she turned round and began to run for the door.

Max caught her before she reached the first cushion. 'You're right,' he said, 'I won't. Faith, I can't be tied down by you or any woman.'

It was too much. He said he loved her, even seemed to mean it in a way, yet he appeared convinced that *her* love was so clinging and dependent that she wouldn't know when to let him go. Wouldn't understand that the call of the mountains was what made him the man he was. She dug her teeth into her lower lip as the need to hurt back became overpowering. Then, since words couldn't get through to him, she lifted her hand and aimed a blow at his face. At that moment it seemed her only option.

But even that satisfaction was denied her.

Without appearing to move, Max caught her wrist and pulled her into his arms.

'No,' he said, 'that won't solve anything, Duchess.'

Faith stared at the black sweatshirt, felt his hard hands on her back. It was true. Hitting him *wouldn't* solve anything. Because according to him there wasn't a solution.

After a while, and without attempting to take things any further, Max let her go. 'Have you settled down now?' he asked, as if he were talking to a child.

Faith thought of telling him just who she'd like to settle, and how, but the urge to hit back at him was fading. After a moment it was gone altogether, to be replaced by a hollow numbness that left her limp and barely able to feel.

'Perhaps you'd better go now,' she said dully. There was no point in prolonging this painful scene.

'You're angry,' he said, not moving.

'Yes, I was. Shouldn't I be?'

'Does it help?'

'Yes, it does,' said Faith. The numbness didn't last long, and she began to feel again, a raw, agonising ache that hurt far more than any physical wound. 'It helps by reminding me that I've fallen in love with a man who pretends to love me back, yet gives me no credit for understanding he has to do the thing he does best. A man who uses his precious freedom as an excuse to avoid any kind of commitment. Who puts himself first and foremost. That's not love, Max. That's running away.'

'That's the second time you've accused me of running away. I don't like it, Duchess.'

'You weren't meant to. But it's the truth, isn't it?'

For a moment, as she saw his fists ball against his thighs, she thought he meant to deny it. Then he straightened his shoulders, tightened his jaw, and said in a voice from which all feeling was explicitly erased, 'Maybe it is. If that's what you want to believe.'

'It doesn't matter what I believe, does it? You're still going. You're not going to give us a chance.'

'There are no chances, Faith. Not for us.'

The words were unequivocal, spoken with a rough finality. But somehow Faith was left with a faint ripple of hope.

'Why not?' she asked. 'You said you loved me.'

'Yes,' he said. 'That's why I'm leaving. *Because* I love you.'

'That makes no sense, Max.' She straightened her shoulders. 'I'm not asking you to give up the life you love. I'm not some clinging vine who needs to be with you every minute of the day.' She laughed bleakly. 'In fact, if I were, we'd probably drive each other crazy.'

'Very likely. Nonetheless, the question is academic. I'm not going to marry you, Faith, and I'm not making you any kind of promise—except to say that when I leave this room it will be the last time you see me. One day I believe you'll be grateful.'

'Shouldn't I be the judge of that?'

'No,' he said harshly, brushing a hand over his forehead, which was beaded with moisture. 'You shouldn't. I make my own decisions. I always have.'

'I see.'

He took a deep breath. 'No, you don't. But believe me, I know what I'm doing.'

Did he? Did he know he was tearing her apart? She stared at him, standing a few feet away from her now, with his legs apart and his jaw lifted aggressively. As if he were taking on the world instead of one grief-stricken woman. Yes, probably he knew exactly what he was doing. He was breaking her heart. And for all his protestations, he didn't care. Not really. His own needs, as always, came first. And she wasn't going to stand here any longer letting him destroy the last vestiges of her pride.

'I'm sure you know what you're doing,' she said coldly. 'And so do I. Get out, Max. Now.'

She knew a small, cheerless satisfaction when he looked stunned—almost as if she'd actually hit him. He hadn't expected that. Had he expected to leave on his own terms, then—and in his own good time?

After a moment he shook his head as if he were trying to clear it, and his eyes became unreadable again. When he moved towards her, Faith had no idea what to expect, but a sixth sense made her step backwards.

'All right,' he said, his voice grating on her already strung-out nerves. 'All right, Duchess. But not before we've said goodbye.'

'I—Max, there's no point...' She took another step backwards and tripped over a nest of cushions. Before she could recover her balance, Max had pulled her into his arms.

Very briefly, he stiffened and stood quite still, and she thought he meant to let her go. But when she raised her eyes to his face, he swore softly and pressed his lips over hers.

He kissed her then with such savage ferocity that the breath was drawn out of her lungs. But this time she felt no response, no instant flicker of desire—because she sensed that he was deliberately trying to hurt her, as he had never hurt her before. But it made no difference. Whatever happened in the future, even if she never saw him again, this man would always be a part of her being. Not even his callous dismissal of their love could alter that.

She tried to escape, but he wouldn't release her, and she let herself go limp in his arms as he moved his mouth to her neck and trailed rough kisses to the base of her throat. His hands were on her hips, pulling her against the hard flatness of his stomach. And then, somehow, they had fallen to the floor and she knew that, even though Max was leaving her, he wanted her as much as he always had.

And he wasn't going to get her. *He* might believe that the passion he felt for her was love, but it wasn't. Gathering up the last remaining threads of her pride, she grasped his hair in her hands and pushed him away.

When she squirmed from his embrace and struggled on to her feet he made no effort to stop her.

He lay sprawled on the floor, staring up at her, his smoky eyes distant and opaque. Then he too rose to his feet and, facing her, drew a finger lightly across her cheek. 'Goodbye, Duchess,' he said quietly. 'And— thank you.'

She blinked. His voice held no trace of passion, was almost cold, but—surely that wasn't moisture in his eyes? No, it couldn't have been, because when she looked again his expression was flat and dismissive, as if that interlude on the floor had never happened.

Then, incredibly, he was taking her hand, giving it a brisk farewell shake before turning to pick up his holdall, which she saw was already propped beside the door.

Faith, her face the colour of pallid wax, stared at his back as he hoisted the bag on to his shoulder and, without a backward glance, strode with brutal resolution out of her life.

She lifted her hand in a useless gesture of farewell, then let it drop back to her side.

Her mountain man was going back to the ice-covered slopes where he belonged.

Jane Farraday had the front door open before Faith even reached the step. 'What happened between you and Max?' she demanded.

'Nothing happened.' Faith moved her mother gently aside. 'He left, that's all.'

'I know. He came round to say goodbye to us.'

'He did?' Faith paused on her way to the living-room, her back rigid.

'Yes, he did. He's going to get in touch with Bruce. Oh, did I tell you Bruce is sharing an apartment with Mike Spender? They were at school together, remember? And he's signed up for a mineralogy course.' When Faith said nothing, Jane took her arm and added, 'That's not what you want to hear about, is it?'

'Of course I do...' Faith pulled away and hurried into the living-room, hoping her father would be there to act as a buffer between her and her mother's questions.

He was just removing a disc from the stereo.

'Frank,' said Jane, 'we have to talk to Faith about Max.'

So much for the buffer. It had just been headed off at the pass. If she hadn't felt like crying, Faith would have laughed.

'What about Max?' she asked drearily, deciding to get the inquisition over.

'Why did you two break up?'

'We were never a pair.' Faith slumped down in the pink velvet chair. 'And there was never any question of— well, of—— '

'Marriage,' said Jane grimly.

'Yes. No. I mean, Max says he'll never get married.'

'Can't blame him,' said Frank, loading another disc in the stereo. 'It's a risky business he's in.'

'You don't know anything about it, Frank,' said Jane dismissively. 'Lots of mountaineers get married.'

'Well, Max won't,' said Faith flatly. Sometimes her mother reminded her of a dog worrying away at a bone. It was easier to let her finish the job. 'He doesn't love me.'

'Did he tell you that?'

'No. *He* said he loves me. But if he meant it, he wouldn't have walked out the way he did.' She tried to smile bravely and couldn't.

'Why would he say it if he doesn't mean it?'

'He doesn't know he doesn't mean it.'

Frank put the disc absently back in its box. 'You're not making any sense. Max struck me as a man who knows his mind better than most. Likes opera too.'

'Yes, but that's not the same thing. He *thinks* he loves me, but he doesn't want any kind of commitment or responsibility. So he ran away. That's not love.'

Frank took the disc out again. 'Bunk.'

Faith blinked. 'What?'

'I said bunk. That man's never run away from a challenge in his life. Look at what he does for a living. Look at what he did in the fire. If he left you, you can bet your boots he wasn't thinking of himself——'

'Then who was he thinking of?'

Frank looked at her as if he suspected he'd given life to an imbecile. 'You, of course. He ought to know better than anyone the kind of risks he takes, and he doesn't want to inflict them on the woman he loves. Probably doesn't figure he has the right.'

Faith stared. Her father always seemed to live in such a dream world, but—maybe he was more perceptive than she thought. Max had told her she deserved a man who didn't risk his neck as a way of life, but she had thought he was thinking mainly of his own freedom. He'd more or less said that was it...

'If you're right, Dad,' she said slowly, 'if you're right, then maybe I shouldn't have let him go without a fight.' Her eyes glazed over.

Ever since Max had left her she had been moving through her days like a zombie. Angela had made a number of baleful comments about secretaries who kept falling in love, and done a lot of eye-rolling, so she had felt obliged to make some sort of effort at work. But once evening came she spent long hours alone on the beach with her banjo, staring out to sea and not playing so much as a note. She felt lost, rudderless, like a ghost ship gliding on an empty ocean. And up until this moment, she had allowed herself to be borne along by the tide. But her father's words had brought a halt to her mindless drifting, and suddenly she had a sense that if she didn't give up, and really believed that she and Max could have a future, then maybe, just maybe, she could make it happen.

'I'm going to Seattle,' she said abruptly.

'Now?' exclaimed Jane, horrified. 'But I've just put lunch in the oven——'

'After lunch,' said Faith, who hadn't totally lost her perspective. 'Come on, I'll help you set the table.'

Three hours later Faith, driving her mother's ancient Volvo, was barrelling down the highway to Seattle.

Much later, long after dark, she parked the car on the side of the steep hill where Bruce and Mike shared a basement apartment, and crossed the road to press a bell marked 'Spender'.

There was no answer, so she pressed it again. Hard. It had a very loud ring.

The fourth time she tried, an irate head appeared from an upstairs window and told her that if she didn't get her finger off that damned bell, he, the owner of the head, would come down and take it off for her.

Faith got her finger off.

Now what? Bruce and Mike were obviously out, and she needed somewhere to put her luggage until she was able to find out from them where Max was staying. If they knew.

She stood with her hand on the steel rail that ran in front of the apartment and stared doubtfully down the brightly lit street. Then she started, closed her eyes, and opened them again disbelievingly.

Surely that figure walking slowly up the hill with his arm round a girl's waist as he bent to whisper into her ear—surely that wasn't...

But it was. She could see the brown lights in his hair clearly in the glow from the street light, and there was no mistaking that strong, aggressive chin, or the catlike walk.

The girl with him was crying.

Dear God. Faith felt a burning sensation in her chest. Was he breaking someone else's heart already? It was too much...

Without realising she was doing it, she made a sound like an animal that had been stepped on, and ran across the road to her car.

Vaguely, as she ran, she was aware of the headlights of another car. They were bright and they made her close her eyes, which were already blinded by tears. Then, again only vaguely, she heard the screech of tyres on pavement, felt a sharp pain in her side, and suddenly she seemed to be flying.

After that she didn't feel anything until she woke up in a hospital bed.

CHAPTER TEN

A WHITE-UNIFORMED figure, slightly blurred, was standing on the periphery of her vision. Faith wasn't sure if it was male or female, but it seemed to be adjusting something which after a while she realised was an intravenous tube.

'Why am I here? Wh-what's happened to me?' she whispered.

'Don't worry, nothing permanent. You had a bit of an argument with a car.' The voice was female and briskly sympathetic.

'Oh. I guess I lost it,' Faith tried to smile, but found it to much of an effort.

'You sure did. Knocked out cold, you were. But that man of yours must have moved like greased lightning, because I'm told he had an ambulance on hand almost before you hit the ground.'

'Man?' said Faith faintly, feeling as though someone was practising a drumroll on her brain.

'Yup. Big guy with wavy brown hair. He's been in and out driving us all crazy ever since you were checked in.'

'Max,' said Faith. And then, not wanting to deal with the thought of Max just yet, 'How long have I been here?'

'Since yesterday. Did a good job on yourself, didn't you?'

'I guess I did. Have I been unconscious all this time?'

'Not exactly. We kept you sedated.'

'My parents...?'

'They'll be back again later.'

'Oh. Does that mean I can go home?'

'In a couple of days. You haven't broken anything that shows, but you're bruised and badly shaken up. That was quite a cut you gave yourself on the head.'

Faith shut her eyes. She knew about that cut because her head was hurting like hell. Perhaps though, if she could just sleep some more...

When she woke again the tube was gone from her arm, the room was clearly in focus, and Max was standing beside the bed looking haggard, unshaven and grim. For a moment, when he saw that she was awake, his eyes met hers with such a blaze of relief that she wanted to reach out and pull him down beside her. But as soon as he saw her smile his face closed up again, and Faith remembered the girl who had been crying in his arms.

'Go away,' she said.

'Faith——'

'Go away.'

'I will in a minute.' She saw his chest rise and knew he was trying to control his temper. 'First tell me what the devil you thought you were doing?'

'Doing?'

'Running into the road like that, in front of a car.'

'I didn't see the car. I was just—running.'

'Why?' His voice was hard, abrasive.

'I don't know. I saw you with that girl, and I ran.'

'Girl? What girl? Oh, *that*.' He was apparently talking to himself now, and suddenly Faith couldn't bear his presence any longer. It hurt too much. More even than the dull ache that seemed to have turned into her head.

'Please go away,' she repeated, and was horrified to feel tears welling up. One trickled slowly down her cheek, and she closed her eyes quickly.

'You're crying,' said Max. He sounded angry. 'Faith, for God's sake——'

'Please,' she whispered. 'Please, Max.' Her fingers clutched at the sheet, began to twist it convulsively.

A shuttered look came over his face. 'OK, Duchess,' he growled, shoving his hands deep into the pockets of his trousers, 'you win.'

He turned on his heel and was gone so quickly that only the sound of his shoes slamming on the hard hospital floor convinced her he had ever been in the room.

There was a taste like sour apples in her mouth, and Faith didn't feel as if she'd won anything.

Max didn't come back, and two days later her parents arrived to take her home.

Faith sat at her kitchen table staring out at the rain-washed mountains and wishing that Angela would allow her to go back to work. At least with her job to occupy her days, she would be forced to keep her mind off all she'd lost. But Angela said no, secretaries with faces that looked as dismal as drizzle at a picnic were bad for business, and anyway Faith needed the rest.

Faith didn't need the rest, but she knew Angela meant to be kind.

She had been home a month now, and had finally convinced her mother that she was sufficiently recovered to return to her own apartment. Max hadn't made any attempt to contact her during her convalescence. She had told him to go away that day in the hospital, and for once, uncharacteristically, he had done exactly as she asked.

A few days ago she had seen him being interviewed on TV, and watching his beloved face, seeing him smile at an entranced female interviewer, had been unbearably painful. More than she could take. In the end she had turned the set off, and felt as if she were turning off her life.

She knew she ought to be thankful Max had stayed away, because all her doubts about him had been confirmed by that glimpse of the weeping girl in his arms. Only days earlier he had said he loved her. But she should have known that with Max it was a matter of out of sight, out of mind. He attracted women like pins to a magnet—as he had automatically attracted Nellie. She should have learned from that incident.

She hadn't, though, and as a result she was lost, desolate and lonely, mourning the loss of Max as she had never mourned the loss of Stephen, and yet furious with him for being the cause of her grief.

Faith focused her gaze on the dark green of the trees carpeting the lower slopes of the mountains, and knew that soon she would have to pick up the pieces of herself and get on with what was left of her life.

A gust of wind rattled the window. She frowned and watched rain begin to streak down the glass. So another summer storm was under way.

Her eyes misted over. It had been stormy the day she met Max. She remembered the deep sound of his voice startling her, making her jump...

She hadn't played a note since she left Seattle.

Faith sat up abruptly. Was she going to let memories of Max deprive her of her music too? The music that had brought peace to her heart in the past, and would again?

No, she was not. Lifting her chin, she marched into the bedroom, grabbed the banjo, and sat down on the edge of her bed to play.

Mrs Gruber, who wasn't in her usual fighting form, waited a full ten minutes before pounding on the ceiling with her broom.

Faith's fingers stilled. It had never been worth antagonising Mrs Gruber. She always retaliated by commenting to Jane that dear Faith didn't seem *quite* herself, and did Jane think she was eating properly?

Sighing, Faith laid down her instrument and went to check on the storm. Clouds, grey and uninviting, hung low in the sky, and the branches of the trees outside her window were tossing back and forth in the wind.

But the rain had stopped, at least for a while. And she had a ghost to lay.

She pulled her navy blue suit jacket over a bright yellow sweater and jeans, picked up her banjo again, and made her way down the stairs with a speed born of long practice in evading Mrs Gruber. She managed to close the front door just before her nosy neighbour poked her head out to see who was leaving.

She didn't look any crazier than usual, Max decided. Just a rather ordinary, could-be-pretty-if-she-bothered country blonde, sitting on a log at the edge of the ocean playing the banjo. In a navy blue suit jacket and jeans— with the looming clouds overhead threatening to release their burden at any moment. The wind whistling past her ears was blowing her long hair across her face like tangled silk . . .

Max closed his eyes. He had been here before, but the scene had shifted subtly. This time he had known he would find her.

Not only Faith's clothing had changed in the weeks since he had first seen her sitting alone on her log, and been forever enchanted—and if he spoke to her now it wasn't sand in the face he envisaged. It was something much more final and more devastating. None the less, he had no choice but to risk it.

Thrusting his hands into the pockets of his jeans, he crunched across the pebbles to where she sat.

'Good evening, Euterpe,' he murmured over her shoulder.

This time Faith didn't jump and say, 'My name's not Euterpe.' Instead she turned, very slowly, put her banjo down and said without raising her voice, 'I came here to *lay* a ghost, not meet one.'

Max's eyes lit with a gleam that he quickly suppressed. His Duchess hadn't changed much after all. 'That could, perhaps, be arranged,' he replied gravely.

A quick spark of anger brought two spots of colour to Faith's cheeks. How dared Max walk out of her life— even at her own request—and then come strolling back into it with a gleam in his eye and a mocking quip on his lips? She had been through weeks of aching pain and loneliness because of him, and she was still fighting desperately to overcome her grief and sense of abandonment. And now here he was, back to overturn the fragile peace she sought. And he was smiling—or trying not to.

'Go away,' she said very distinctly, spelling out all three syllables.

'Not this time.' He moved around the log and sat beside her. 'I only went last time because I was afraid my inflammatory presence would hinder your speedy recovery.'

'It would have.'

'That's what I thought. So I waited until your mother assured me you were up to me——'

'Oh,' said Faith, feeling as if a great lump of lead lay on her chest. 'Well, I'm not up to you. If I'd known you'd come——'

'If you'd known I'd come, you would have told her you were coming down with double pneumonia and a severe case of pimples on the nose. Is that it?'

She gazed bleakly at the crests breaking white over the big, swollen rollers. 'Something like that. Without the pimples.'

'Why, Faith?' He caught her by the elbows and pulled her around to face him. 'I know I hurt you, and I regret that more than you'll ever know. But don't I deserve another chance?'

Faith crushed an unbidden spark of response, ruthlessly, before it could turn into hope. 'Chance to what? Shatter my life again? Make me fall in love with you all over again—because you happen to be in between engagements and can use a nice willing woman?'

'Faith,' said Max, putting a hand on the back of her neck and pulling her face so close to his that she could see the pores, 'I came here to make amends. Keep it up and you could find yourself with yet another grievance to hold against me.' He slid his hand down her spine.

'Oh, sure,' said Faith wearily. 'If you can't get what you want with smiles and charm, you'll resort to more chauvinistic methods. Is that what you mean?'

To her surprise, his shoulders slumped slightly, and he shook his head. For the first time she noticed the lines of strain creasing his forehead and a hollowness in his eyes that spoke of sleepless nights and mornings as lonely as hers. 'No,' he said, 'that's not what I mean. But I haven't had a lot of sleep lately—my own fault, I admit—and patience has never been my strong point. So I'd appreciate it if you'd save the acid until I've had a chance to say what I've come here to say.'

Faith turned away, stared at the waves washing over the sand and felt the first drop of rain fall on her head. An appropriate setting for yet another goodbye, she thought bitterly.

'All right,' she said, 'say it. Ease your conscience, if that's what this is all about.'

She didn't see the flesh pull tight across the bones of his face, because she was still staring grimly out to sea. But she felt him stiffen. And, seconds later, she was conscious of a startling sense of loss as he took his hands from her waist and shifted his body along the log to leave a gaping space in between them.

'It's not about easing my conscience,' he said, in a voice almost as frozen as hers. 'It's about our future.'

'What future? You've already told me we don't have one. That the great mountaineer can't be tied down.'

She heard him draw in his breath. 'I know. But that wasn't the true reason.'

'Oh? What other riveting revelations have you in store for me? Are you about to tell me you were secretly engaged to Nellie? Or to the girl in Seattle, perhaps?'

'Girl in...? Dammit, Faith!' He stood up suddenly and pulled her with him, forcing her to meet his eyes. 'You know damn well I'm not, and never was, engaged, to anyone. I thought of it once, a long time ago, and, like a naïve young fool, I expected my intended would wait patiently at home for me while I trotted off round the globe. But the very first time I left her, I came back to find she'd traded me in on a man with a job in the City. He was buying her a house in the suburbs which he expected to come home to every night.'

Faith eyed his grim visage sceptically. 'I see. And I suppose you decided that was sufficient excuse to abstain from any further attempts at commitment?'

Max dropped her hands and stared stonily over her head. 'No. I came to see that Marilyn had every right to give up on me. She knew better than I did that I didn't love her enough. All the same, losing her hurt like hell. It made me grow up, fast. I realised that I couldn't expect to have my cake and eat it as well. Then I took a good hard look at my parents' marriage. All their lives they were closer to each other than most couples, and very happy. Because they spent time together. My father never went away without my mother, and he never wanted to. They dedicated themselves to each other and to raising their children, and I believed that theirs was the ideal kind of marriage.' He ran the back of his hand across his eyes, and when he spoke again his voice was deeper, less abrasive. 'I couldn't offer a woman anything less than that, Faith, but I had no intention of giving up the only kind of life I knew—or ever wanted to know. It wasn't an excuse to evade responsibility. It was a conscious decision not to put any woman through the risk and the inevitable loneliness of...' he paused, and she saw the muscles moving in his throat '...of loving me.'

'I understand,' said Faith, not seeing where this was leading and wishing Max would get it over with quickly.

Being with him like this was so painful now that she didn't think she could endure it much longer. Because she knew that, whatever he said, this meeting could only end in heartbreak. She looked desperately up at the sky as the wind whipped at her hair and another drop of rain dampened her head.

'No,' said Max, 'I don't think you do understand.'

Faith sighed. 'I understand you're telling me that when you said your freedom was all-important to you it wasn't the whole truth. That in part you were being honourable and altruistic. But it doesn't make sense, Max. Not after what I saw in Seattle. And in any case, what difference does it make? Either way, I lose.' Her voice broke, and she turned away to stare blindly down at the sand.

'Faith?' He came up behind her and wrapped his arms round her waist. 'I don't expect you to believe me, but when I came back from Seattle that day it wasn't just because I owed you the courtesy of a final goodbye. I wanted to see you again, one last time. I don't think I ever meant to let you know I loved you.' She shivered in his arms, and he went on urgently, 'But I did let you know. In the end I couldn't help myself. And I knew then that to be fair to you, I had to do my best to make you see me in the worst possible light——'

'That wasn't hard,' said Faith, struggling not to surrender to the sensuous comfort of his embrace, willing herself not to lean her head back on his chest.

His arms tightened. 'I realise that,' he said. 'But you have to agree that it's much easier to stop loving a man you despise than it is to forget one you respect. I didn't want to hurt you any more than I had already, Duchess. That's why I left you so brutally, and let you believe my love was only superficial. I *wanted* you to hate me.'

'Yes,' said Faith drearily, as a wave crashed almost at her feet, 'I wanted to hate you too. But I couldn't.'

Behind her Max muttered something she didn't hear, and before she realised what he was up to he had scooped her into his arms and was striding across the beach towards the road.

She watched the wind stir his thick hair, paralysed by the feel of his arms around her, and for a moment bereft of thought or speech. Then sanity returned and she gasped faintly, 'Max, my banjo...'

He swore and dumped her upright on to the pebbles. 'Get in the car,' he ordered. 'There's going to be a deluge any minute. I'll get the banjo.'

Still half hypnotised, Faith thought vaguely that she'd played this scene, or one very like it, once before. But Max was right. The storm was by no means over, and any moment it would soak them to the skin.

She climbed up to the road and scrambled into the car.

Max, carrying the banjo, lowered himself beside her just as the first blast of storm-driven rain hurled itself at the windscreen.

Faith tried to keep her eyes straight ahead, but in the end she couldn't resist a glance at his profile. Only it wasn't his profile that met her gaze, but the full force of his penetrating grey eyes.

She turned away quickly, and without a word Max shifted gears and started the engine with a roar that sounded to her like a statement.

When they pulled up in front of her apartment she tried to slide out and make a run for it. But Max stopped her with a hand on her wrist.

'No,' he said. 'I'm coming up with you.'

'Max, there's no point.' She pulled away, slammed the door behind her and hurried through the downpour as if the very devil were in pursuit.

But Max was no devil. He was just a very determined man who wouldn't let her mend her heart in peace.

When she opened the door he put his hand on the small of her back and pushed her in.

'How's Mrs Gruber behaving?' he asked conversationally, as they climbed the stairs past the neighbourhood busybody's door.

Faith resisted an impulse to kick him into silence, and didn't answer until they reached the privacy of her apartment.

'Mrs Gruber's behaving as badly as usual,' she replied tightly. 'And as she undoubtedly heard that remark, by now she'll be thinking up ways to pay us back.'

'What sort of ways?' Max leaned against the door and lifted an eyebrow.

'Ways like telling my mother that...' Faith stopped abruptly. 'Max, what has Mrs Gruber to do with anything?'

'Nothing. I guess I'm trying to put off the moment of truth.'

'Why? What moment of truth?'

He shifted his shoulders against the panelling and stared rigidly at a point above her head. 'The moment when I put my heart and my hopes in your hands. The moment when, if you refuse me, I'll have to face the fact that by my own fatal blindness and arrogance I've lost the most precious gift I've ever had.'

Faith moistened her lips, and stared at him with wide, disbelieving eyes. Did he mean what she thought he meant? If he did, it wasn't apparent from the expressionless mask of his face. 'Gift?' she whispered, holding on to the lapels of her damp jacket. 'What gift, Max?'

His eyes met hers, and the look he gave her was no longer enigmatic, but filled with such passionate intensity that she gasped. 'The gift of your love,' he said simply.

He spoke so directly, with such powerful, soul-deep sincerity, that Faith felt a great pressure in her chest. Her throat was rough and she had a ridiculous sense that at any moment she would burst into tears. Which wouldn't help either of them.

Slowly, stepping very cautiously to avoid the cushions, she backed away from him until she was pressed against the opposite wall. She accepted its support gratefully. 'Max,' she began with great care, attempting not to show any emotion, 'are you trying to tell me——?'

'I'm not trying. I *am* telling you,' he interrupted roughly. 'I love you, Faith. And if you'll have me, I want to marry you.'

'Oh!' Involuntarily her hand flew to her mouth. Now, at last, after she had given up all hope, all expectation, he was saying the words that once she had so longed to hear. And she felt curiously drained, detached, unable to express herself, not sure even what she wanted to say. Because after everything that had gone before, Max's sudden reversal left her confused and more unsure of her own needs and feelings than she had ever been in her life.

'"Oh"?' repeated Max. 'Faith, that's not an answer.'

'No.' She closed her eyes, listened to the soothing murmur of a plane high in the sky above their heads.

'Are you going to give me one?'

She opened her eyes again then, forced herself to look at him, standing there with his arms crossed and his legs a little apart against the door. She thought that if he had any doubts about her answer his face certainly wasn't betraying them now. He looked as carelessly at ease as ever, confident and in charge of his world. And yet he had called her love a precious gift, told her that his heart lay in her hands...

'I don't—don't think I have an answer,' she mumbled, dropping her eyes to a particularly lurid crimson cushion.

She was only vaguely aware that he had left his place by the door, and she didn't realise he had crossed the room until she felt his knuckles beneath her chin, tilting it upwards.

'Faith,' he said quietly, 'you once said you loved me. Do you?'

That one was easy to answer. 'Yes,' she said steadily. 'Yes, Max, I do.'

He nodded. 'That's a start, then. But you're not sure if I'm—good marriage material. Is that it?'

'I suppose so,' she agreed miserably.

'Can't say I blame you.' He released her chin so suddenly that her head dropped forward on to his chest.

She lifted it quickly so she could look directly into his eyes. 'Max, it's not because you climb mountains, or because I know you'll have to go away. It's—it's—that girl. The one you had your arm round in Seattle...' She stopped when she saw his face change suddenly, making him look less careworn and much younger, as if some heavy burden had miraculously fallen off his back.

'Are you saying,' he asked, as though she had just told him he'd won a trip to the moon, 'that the only thing stopping you from saying "yes" is that you saw

me with—what was her name? Tracey, that's it.' He
wiped a hand round the back of his neck. 'Oh, God,
I'm sorry, Duchess. I should have explained at once,
shouldn't I? But it seemed so unimportant compared to
all the very real problems we'll have to face.'

Dear lord, thought Faith, he couldn't even remember
the girl's name. 'Max,' she said, in a voice she had
trouble keeping steady, 'as far as I'm concerned, your
involvement with another woman—even if you can't remember her name—*is* important. And if you think it
isn't, I can't see that there's any hope for us at all.'

Max shook his head impatiently and seized her hands.
'No, Duchess, don't be an idiot. Tracey is Mike Spender's
girlfriend. She had a fight with him and ran off down
the street crying her eyes out and threatening to do
something stupid. Mike was worried about her, and out
of habit Bruce phoned me—he has this crazy idea I work
miracles. Anyway, I said I'd do what I could, and I found
her in the local bar trying to convince the bartender that
she was old enough to be served Bourbon on the rocks.
So I hauled her out of there fast and took her back to
her Mike.' He sighed. 'Or I would have done if you
hadn't interrupted the rescue operation with that suicidal
dash across the road.'

'Oh,' said Faith, feeling as if she'd just been run over
by a tank. A rather sexy tank whose hands gripping hers
were sending familiar messages up her spine. 'Max, you
don't mean...' She stopped, stared at his face, which
had gone very still. 'Do you mean you had your arm
round her like that just to—well, to comfort her? Is that
what you're saying?'

'Yes. And to make sure she didn't try to run away.'
His lips twisted ruefully. 'Which she might have done if

Bruce hadn't shown up in time to see his sister having a head-on with a Mazda.'

Faith swallowed. The tank seemed to have left her dazed and a little squashed, but still alive. And gradually, as the confusion in her head began to settle, she came face to face with the only thing that mattered.

Max loved her. He wanted to marry her. And there was nothing to stop her saying 'yes'.

She said it.

Max drew her towards him until her breasts were just touching his chest. 'Yes?' he asked, hope and wariness reflected in his eyes in equal measure. 'Faith, are you telling me——?'

'I'm telling you "yes". I'll marry you.' When he made no response, but stood gazing at her as if she had said something beyond his comprehension, she added doubtfully, 'You did ask me, didn't you? You haven't changed your mind?'

He moved then, so fast she didn't know what had happened to her until she found herself crushed in an embrace so powerful it left her gasping for breath.

'No, my beloved Duchess,' he murmured into her hair, 'I haven't changed my mind. At least, I suppose I have, but I swear I'll never do it again.'

All Faith wanted then was to give in to the hunger raging within her, to satisfy the longing that had filled her being ever since the terrible day when Max had left her. But there were things that had to be said first.

She put her hands on his chest and tried to push him away. He didn't move. 'Max,' she said, revelling in the lean strength of his body and feeling the thudding of his heart next to hers, 'Max, I'm sorry I thought—thought Tracey was——'

'A replacement for you?' He slid his hands over her hips and rocked her up against him. 'You should be sorry about that. How could you imagine any woman could possibly replace my Duchess?'

'I—I don't...'

He laughed suddenly, and held her against the wall with his palms flat on her shoulders. 'Grovel,' he ordered. 'Show me how sorry you are.'

Unaccountably Faith felt her eyes fill with tears. She wasn't sure why. Partly sheer happiness, she supposed, partly relief from tension. And partly that because now, although she still didn't understand Max's change of heart, she couldn't think how she could ever have doubted his love, or thought him capable of such fickle affection.

'Oh, God,' groaned Max, seeing her tears, 'I didn't mean it, sweetheart. I was only teasing. You have nothing whatever to be sorry for. I *wanted* you to think I was the kind of bastard who's only interested in his own needs and pleasures. Of course you jumped to the wrong conclusions. And when you jumped in front of that car as well, I thought all the decisions I'd taken so long to make had come too late. If you'd died——'

'I didn't die,' Faith pointed out. 'What decisions?'

He took her hands again and pulled her down on to the cushions. Then, after he'd settled his back against the wall, he lifted her on to his thighs.

'I came to see I'd been a blind fool,' he said gruffly, 'and that if I didn't come to my senses quickly and ask you to marry me, I'd have only myself to blame if I was forced to spend the rest of my life alone. Without you, my beautiful Duchess.' He stroked a finger across her cheek, and it wasn't cold, it was warm. 'I also came to understand that I'd never had the right to condemn you to that same fate because of the prejudices *I'd* built up over a lifetime. It's true Marilyn couldn't cope with my lifestyle. But you're not Marilyn. And it's also true that my parents had a wonderful marriage. But theirs isn't the only kind that can work.'

'Do you mean,' Faith interrupted him, not quite believing what she was hearing, 'that you would have come back anyway? Even if I hadn't had that—that head-on with a Mazda?'

'Mmm-hmm.' He slid his hand gently down her back, and outside the rain spattered against the window. 'I'd have come back. But I had a number of commitments to fulfil first. And I was by no means convinced that you'd have me. I'd done my level best to make you hate me, and I thought once you'd had time to think you might very well have come to agree with me that life with a mountaineer would be no...' He stopped suddenly. 'Do you realise your jacket is soaked?'

'Is it?' Faith said vaguely. 'Never mind, Angela isn't around to say I'm bad for business.'

'Maybe not,' said Max. 'But I am. And your jacket is very bad for the kind of business I have in mind.'

'Mmm,' murmured Faith, as he began to unbutton it purposefully, 'I believe you're right. You're sort of damp too. I like it.'

'You'd better like it,' he muttered, removing not only the jacket, but her jeans and his sweater as well.

Some time later, when Max's business had been conducted most satisfactorily, Faith lay on the cushions beneath a blanket. Her head rested on his naked chest and she thought dreamily that she must be the happiest woman in the world. So what if Max wouldn't always be by her side? He was with her now, and she had always accepted what life had to give her without a lot of senseless striving for that which she knew she couldn't have. Max was the one who had to overcome obstacles instead of finding a way around them, who would always seek new mountains to conquer. And that was good. They were a team. They would complement one another.

'What are you thinking?' he asked softly, stroking his fingers through her hair.

'I'm thinking that you and I make a good team.'

'Yes,' he agreed, 'that's the conclusion I came to once I'd got over thinking that every marriage had to be a carbon copy of my parents'. And it's a fact that not any woman *could* put up with me—or with the kind of life I lead. But you're different, aren't you, Duchess?' He patted her thigh. 'You're content with what you have, without in any way allowing people like me to take advantage of you. You know who and what you are, and you understand that I have to be what I am. I should have known that right from the beginning.' He laughed wryly and kneaded her shoulder. 'Maybe I did know. I remember being knocked for a loop the moment I saw a crazy lady with a banjo sitting on the beach in a rainstorm. It wasn't until that day we went to Hoh, though, that I was certain something was happening to both of us, and that sooner or later I'd have to face it and deal with it.'

Faith smiled and put a hand to his cheek. 'You were horrible at Hoh. I think I knew *you* were the one and only when I found you cooking up Bodger's Stew. Any man who could live on that——'

'It was the only antidote I could think of to lupins,' explained Max, gazing pensively up at the ceiling.

'Geraniums,' said Faith. She raised herself on her elbow and laughed down at him. 'On second thoughts, perhaps it wasn't Bodger's that did it. It was the look on Dad's face when you told him you'd grown up on opera. I knew he'd fallen for you in a big way, and I guess I've always followed his example.'

'Have you? So that's why you sit on beaches playing your music to the fish. It's the same sort of thing as conducting an orchestra made up of chairs.'

'I suppose so. Max...?'

'Mmm?'

She trailed a lock of her hair across his nose. 'Where are we going to live once we're married? You said yourself you don't have any permanent roots, and——'

'I hoped,' he interrupted, tracing a finger along her lower lip, 'that for a while at least you might consider uprooting yourself along with me. I've been asked to lead an expedition to the Andes.'

Faith blinked. 'You want us to live in the Andes?'

He sat up again to pull on his trousers. 'I do believe you would if I asked you to,' he said, smiling. 'No, Duchess, not permanently. Two of the team are bringing their wives along, so how would you feel about coming too? You could stay at base camp. I realise it's an odd sort of honeymoon...'

Faith's heart leaped. Max didn't plan to leave her behind. Some day, in the not-too-distant future, he might have to. But not yet. And, with him, she suspected any kind of honeymoon would be odd. Odd, exciting and magical.

'I'd feel wonderful about it,' she said, wrapping herself in a blanket. 'Provided, of course, that you promise not to break your neck on some precipice while I'm waiting patiently below.'

Max reached for his shirt and stood up. 'I haven't so far,' he pointed out. 'Had some close calls, I'll admit. But knowing you're down there waiting for me—did you say patiently?—will be enough to stop me from taking risks.'

'No, it won't,' said Faith, smiling up at him. 'Taking risks is what you do.'

Max grinned. 'All right, I won't take any *needless* risks,' he amended.

She sighed. 'I suppose that's the best I can hope for. So when do we leave?'

'That's what I like about you, Duchess.' He held out his hand to pull her up beside him. 'Always direct and to the point. I don't know about you, but *I* was thinking of getting married first.'

'So was I,' said Faith. 'How about next weekend?'

'How about tomorrow?' It wasn't a suggestion, it was a statement of exactly what he meant to happen.

'We need a licence.'

'I have one.'

'I thought you said you weren't sure of me?'

'I wasn't.' His smile was wryly derisive. 'But one thing my kind of life has taught me is always to be prepared for the unlikely.'

Faith touched a hand to his cheek. 'Did you really think I was unlikely?' she asked, watching the creases fan out around his eyes.

'Yes, as well as improbable, impossible and un-predictable.'

'Oh,' said Faith. She thought for a moment. 'Well, so are you. And you haven't answered my question.'

'What question?'

'Where are we going to live? After South America?'

'Does it matter?' He frowned slightly.

'No, not really...'

'Then I see no reason why you shouldn't travel with me most of the time. Until the kids are old enough for school——'

'Kids?' interrupted Faith, her voice rising.

'Just two of them.' He smiled imperturbably. 'By that time we'll have bought us our own base camp. Maybe right here in Caley Cove. After we've visited my mother in Scotland, of course. And I'll come home as often as I can. And you'll come with me as often as *you* can——'

'And all the comings and goings will give Molly Bracken, Clara Malone and Mrs Gruber a whole new interest in life,' Faith murmured into his neck.

'Hmm.'

'Hmm what?' She didn't trust that contemplative glitter in his eye.

He didn't answer, and a moment later she knew she'd had good reason to be suspicious.

With a decisive nod Max moved her aside, strode to the front door and shouted into the hall and down the stairs, 'Mrs Gruber, do I have news for you! The Duchess and I are getting married. Tomorrow. By special licence. Honeymoon in South America. Children to follow—two of them. Got that? Two. Eventual home possibly Caley Cove. Pass the word around, will you? Over and out.'

A door slammed downstairs and, very faintly, they heard the sound of urgent dialling coming from the apartment below.

Faith, almost but not quite speechless, grabbed his arm. 'Are you crazy?' she spluttered. 'If she isn't calling the police to arrest you for disturbing the peace, it'll be all over town in five minutes. It will anyway.'

'I know. That's the general idea. I *want* the whole world to know. Besides, it will save us time in the long run. Time that can be much better spent in other, more—invigorating ways.' Max put his hands on her hips and cast a meaningful look at the cushions they had so recently abandoned. 'Don't you agree?'

Faith gave a gurgle of laughter and collapsed helplessly into his arms.

Max was right. Mrs Gruber could spread the news. There were *much* better ways to pass the time.

Harlequin Romance ®

New from Harlequin Romance
a very special six-book series by

MIDNIGHT SONS

DEBBIE MACOMBER

The town of Hard Luck, Alaska, needs women!

The O'Halloran brothers, who run a bush-plane service called Midnight Sons, are heading a campaign to attract women to Hard Luck. *(Location: north of the Arctic Circle. Population: 150—mostly men!)*

"Debbie Macomber's *Midnight Sons* series is a delightful romantic saga. And each book is a powerful, engaging story in its own right. Unforgettable!"

—Linda Lael Miller

TITLE IN THE MIDNIGHT SONS SERIES:

Harlequin Romance ®

brings you

Some men are worth waiting for!

They're handsome, they're charming but, best of all, they're single! Twelve lucky women are about to discover that finding Mr. Right is not a problem—it's holding on to him.

In May the series continues with:

#3408 MOVING IN WITH ADAM
by Jeanne Allan

Hold out for Harlequin Romance's heroes in coming months...

♦ June: THE DADDY TRAP—Leigh Michaels
♦ July: THE BACHELOR'S WEDDING—Betty Neels
♦ August: KIT AND THE COWBOY—Rebecca Winters

HOFH-5

BRIDE'S
BAY RESORT

UNLOCK THE DOOR TO GREAT ROMANCE
AT BRIDE'S BAY RESORT

Join Harlequin's new across-the-lines series, set
in an exclusive hotel on an island off the coast of
South Carolina.

Seven of your favorite authors will bring you exciting stories
about fascinating heroes and heroines discovering love at
Bride's Bay Resort.

Look for these fabulous stories coming to a store near you
beginning in January 1996.

Harlequin American Romance #613 in January
Matchmaking Baby by Cathy Gillen Thacker

Harlequin Presents #1794 in February
Indiscretions by Robyn Donald

Harlequin Intrigue #362 in March
Love and Lies by Dawn Stewardson

Harlequin Romance #3404 in April
Make Believe Engagement by Day Leclaire

Harlequin Temptation #588 in May
Stranger in the Night by Roseanne Williams

Harlequin Superromance #695 in June
Married to a Stranger by Connie Bennett

Harlequin Historicals #324 in July
Dulcie's Gift by Ruth Langan

Visit Bride's Bay Resort each month wherever
Harlequin books are sold.

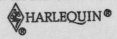

HARLEQUIN ®

BBAYG